Heroes in Education

A New Perspective for Dedicated Individuals in
Public Schools

Philip Brent Gonzalez

Dedication

I will never forget hearing time and time again from various teaching and administrative personnel in our public-school system who have 15 to 30 years of experience; *"Nobody cares, and nobody says thank you for what we deal with."*

That perception and attitude need to be changed. This book was inspired by all of you who work in our public-school system, my experience working with you, and the teachers who encouraged me when I was a K-12 student. My goal is to empower you because you are the pillar of influence for our youth, and the influence of educators on students has led to many great successes in American society.

Your efforts and sacrifice to serve the public are commendable, and I had no idea how little appreciation is shown. I conclude as you might as a reader also concur that these individuals are the *real* heroes of the modern era. I'm a veteran, and I have been told: *"Thank you for your service"* plenty of times. It is true; we must thank veterans, first responders, police officers, and firefighters. They are real-life heroes, and there is no doubt about it. But it is time to also express our gratitude to those who work in our public schools. Regardless of whether you are a teacher or an administrator, this book is for you.

Acknowledgment

I would like to thank my family, friends, and faculty who supported me during this project. Your dedication, objectivity, and passion for education are unwavering.

About the Author

To be honest, I'd rather keep this short because this book is about others. Instead of diving into my entire background, I'd rather just discuss why I have such a passion for the field of education. After serving in the U.S. military for eight years and being honorably discharged, I had an opportunity to pursue a college education. Not knowing the direction my life would go, I found my passion in graduate school in the field of public administration. Because of this passion, I then began to pursue my Ph.D. in education policy.

After graduate school, I started working as an adjunct professor and have had a lot of success, including a good reputation on campus. But almost all the courses are offered at night, and I needed a job during the day. I also wanted to expand my parameters as an instructor and challenge myself, so I could be a better leader to students. I took on a position as a substitute teacher for two years at a local inner-city high school. Believe me, the challenge I sought came full circle, but my experience was invaluable, and I met some of the most dedicated administrators and passionate teachers that I could ever have the honor of knowing. I learned a lot about the ins and outs of the public school system, along with its pros and cons. Needless to say, I also have gained extensive knowledge on this subject matter due to my post-graduate education, which certainly provided a great compass. I was exposed on the front lines of issues of inequality among youth, which I will discuss in this book. To summarize, I am passionate about education, because those who work in this field have a heart of gold and are the greatest heroes of our society.

Contents

Page Left Blank Intentionally

Chapter 1
Introduction

*"Teachers are out there with a very difficult job,
which they pursue with tireless dedication."*

–Chi McBride

According to the Pew Research Center[1], U.S. primary school children spend an average of 943 hours in the classroom each year, while secondary schoolchildren receive another 1,016 hours of instructional time. These children will have spent about 11,700 hours of their lives (more than 12,000 if they attended kindergarten) learning from various teachers by the time they leave high school.

Those 12,000 or 11,700 hours are sizable – remember when a school year used to feel like an eternity? This is because no real accounting has been done by authorities of the total number of time students spend in classrooms (from kindergarten

---

[1]Drew Desilver, September 2014, School days: How the U.S. compares with other countries:https://www.pewresearch.org/fact-tank/2014/09/02/school-days-how-the-u-s-compares-with-other-countries/

through professional education or university). Consider this as well: The National Center for Educational Statistics surmised that nearly 50.7 million kids were enrolled in elementary and secondary public schools in fall 2019[2]. On top of that number, there are 5.2 million kids who attend private schools. How many kids are in one public school classroom? The average number of kids per classroom is just over 26[3], and many teachers attest their classrooms are overcapacity. Usually, there is no aid offered, and other help also is in short supply. It's a tough exercise to qualify those numbers, but one could say that in a year, the average classroom supports over 25,000 hours of learning carried out by dedicated teachers.

You could also take the philosophical route, and ask this question: What do teachers make for all this work? To be honest, most teachers will say not much considering they regularly spend the evening emailing parents and guardians and developing the state standard lesson plan. Also, there is pressure to help

---

[2]https://nces.ed.gov/fastfacts/display.asp?Id=372
[3]https://nces.ed.gov/surveys/sass/tables/sass1112_2013314_t1s_007.asp

kids learn more from their teachers than how to read and write. Teachers are now expected to help kids learn such life skills as how to analyze, make proper decisions, conflict resolution techniques, and negotiation tactics.[4] Given the fact it's a teacher's job to not only give kids the tools they need to become productive members of society... we should be asking whether we are giving our teachers the appreciation they rightly deserve. I believe it's not even close.

Teachers and administrators do their best when it comes to tending to the needs of struggling kids. Yet also know for a fact that the bridge of inequality that divides the good students from the struggling will always remain the same. To get an idea, imagine the following case scenario: Suppose you are a teacher in a high school classroom in a typical U.S. public school. Every day, after the end of classes for the day, the students rush up from their seats and line at the classroom door so that they can leave early. However, in the class, next door, honor, and AP students are busy

---

[4]Suzanne Capek Tingley, The Roles of Teachers Outside of Classroom:https://www.wgu.edu/heyteach/article/roles-teachers-outside-classroom-finding-balance-between-teaching-and-your-extra-duties1807.html

discussing something interesting and productive that only ends up after the bell rings. Lunchtime begins, and after it, a few of those students attend class at a local junior college. These students earn high school and higher-education credits at the same time. Where does inequality in education arrive? Some of these high-achievers who take AP classes might return home in the evening to take an online college course, which will help them get further ahead in their educational endeavors and life.

These kids don't have any distractions or disruptions at home. They also have the peace in which to study and most likely have supportive parents or guardians who can afford additional help. Meanwhile, back at school, the struggling kids are either taking a remedial class or are behind in their studies because they don't have an internet connection at home or any other reason why that child is taking a remedial class.[5]

---

[5]Eric Jensen, How Poverty Affects Classroom Engagement:
http://www.ascd.org/publications/educational-leadership/may13/vol70/num08/How-Poverty-Affects-Classroom-Engagement.aspx

After all, chances are advanced students are meeting with their SAT tutors over the weekend, while their not-so-fortunate classmates may be working. I have seen students working at many local businesses. Though we can be pleased to see these kids working and contributing as a member of society early on in life, those of us who are passionate about education know we want to see these kids meet their full potential academically and eventually pursue attainable goals.

Although these students are the same when it comes to sharing a school building and facilities offered, they also form a separate – and privileged – population, which is common in the country. The differences between the advantaged and disadvantaged, are the same that are between public and private schools when it comes to social disparity and inequality.

Though we can conclude it's due to the availability of funds, equitable resources, and stable home life for kids in private schools, this is an entirely different discussion that I do not want to delve into because my focus is on the public-school system. To put it simply, I want to communicate through this book how society has and continues to put a great number of expectations on our public schools.[6] This is understandable since it is the most important aspect of our society that involves our youth. However, through research, you will discover that my argument is to purport the philosophy and encourage everyone to show greater appreciation for those who work in our public schools.

Though some social inequality issues are on the rise and can be challenging, there also are some successes that I believe are due to the great men and women who positively influence our youth. As a result, it has made these occupations more demanding.

To put it simply, teachers, substitute teachers, and administrators are the true heroes of our society because they help fight inequality. For instance, being a teacher once meant teaching and mentoring students academically. The role has changed, and though this primary responsibility as a teacher is still practiced, teachers must now have a vast and flexible

---

[6]David N. Plank, Understanding the Need for Schooling: http://www.oecd.org/education/ceri/35393937.pdf

instructional approach to reflect the ever-changing diversity of their students. This also applies to the Principals and their staff. Without leadership, teachers cannot instill the structure that is needed in our schools.

We need to find a way to bridge the gap of social inequality that is prevalent in American public schools. This can only be done after first understanding the issues faced by students. I ask you as a reader not to perceive the information provided in a negative light. Instead, readers should view the material as a tool to show how much we need to express our thanks to you regardless of what role you play in our public schools.

Believe me… there are many pieces of literature, journals, and news coverage that discuss the negative aspects of our schools. But that is not what this book is about. This book is about getting to the core of what educators accomplish in their roles in our public schools that is underappreciated. I believe there is a great need to turn the tide of our public perception in a positive direction. This book is meant to say: *"Thank You, We Appreciate You because you are the true heroes of American society."*

America's Youth and Their Losing Fight with Social Issues[7]

As per a Pew Research Center survey[8], American teens think about many things that concern them directly, in addition to having a lot on their plates. Who wouldn't when they have so much to deal with on a near-daily basis? Substantial research points to anxiety, drug abuse, depression, and bullying as some of the major problems youth ages 13 to 17 face every day.

These problems pave a bumpy road to other problems and are more often than not connected to poverty, homelessness, and dysfunctional family life. Just how common are these issues and the negative experiences that crop up as a result of teens in the U.S.? The following is the most recent data available from researchers and state departments regarding the issues faced by American youth.

---

[7] Major Issues Facing Teenagers:
https://www.zurinstitute.com/issues-facing-teenagers/

[8] Juliana Menasce Horowitz& Nikki Graf, February 2019, Most U.S. Teens See Anxiety and Depression as a Major Problem among Their Peers: https://www.pewsocialtrends.org/2019/02/20/most-u-s-teens-see-anxiety-and-depression-as-a-major-problem-among-their-peers/

Anxiety and Depression

In a sad state of affairs, serious mental health is the number 1 concern shared by many American teens. A survey conducted by the Pew Research Center shows seven (in ten) teens said depression and anxiety are major problems they face. Mental health researchers and clinicians have the same concern for the youth of this country.

The condition is so prevalent in teens as per a national survey reporting children's health, 7% of youth between the ages of 3 and 17 suffered from anxiety and depression from 2016 to 2017.[9] Meanwhile, more teens have been reporting serious depression for the past several years,[10]

As per a national survey on drug use and health, in 2016, about 12.8% of youth who were between ages 12 to 17 said they had undergone a serious intensity depressive episode in the past year, which had increased by 8% in 2010. Severe impairment issues

---

[9]https://www.childhealthdata.org/browse/survey

[10]Rebecca ahrnsbrakjonaki Bose Sarra L. Hedden Rachel N. Lipari Eunice Park-Lee, September 2017, Key Substance Use and Mental Health Indicators in the United States: Results from the 2016 National Survey on Drug Use and Health:https://www.samhsa.gov/data/sites/default/files/NSDUH-FFR1-2016/NSDUH-FFR1-2016.pdf

were also noted by 9% of youths. Additionally, very few of those teens had been treated for the conditions and the after-effects of depression.

Drugs/Alcohol Addiction

Sadly, the American youth of today don't only have to face issues such as anxiety and depression as per a survey. The Pew Research Center reports that addiction to drugs and alcohol also comes under major concerns that aren't being addressed adequately.

However, fewer teens are drinking alcohol, according to a survey by Monitoring the Future[11], a long-running program of the University of Michigan. It also found that teens are forced by peer pressure when it comes to imbibing in alcohol and drugs. In 2017, 30.2% of 12th graders and 18.6% of 10th graders had drunk alcohol in the past month. The numbers have significantly gone down over the span of three decades. However, 16% of teens in Pew's survey reported feeling "a lot" or "some" strain from peers to

---

[11]Miech, R. A., Schulenberg, J. E., Johnston, L. D., Bachman, J. G., O'Malley, P. M., & Patrick, M. E. (December 17, 2018). "National Adolescent Drug Trends in 2018: http://monitoringthefuture.org/data/18data.html#2018data-drugs

drink alcohol. What about drug abuse? According to the ongoing Monitoring the Future survey, the use of marijuana is nearly as high as it was two decades ago among 12thgraders. In 2017, 22.2% of teens reported using marijuana for recreation and stress relief in the past 30 days versus 22.8% in 1998.

In fact, its usage has always been the most commonly used drug among teens. More than 10% of 12th graders reported having another drug than marijuana in the late 1990s and early 2000s, but the figure is 6% now for that particular age group.

Bullying and Cyberbullying

As per a survey by the Pew Research Center, many people find name-calling and rumor-spreading to be incredibly unpleasant and challenging aspects of adolescent life. It's difficult to deal with such situations. The rise of social media and the rapid incorporation of smartphones in our daily lives have transformed when, where, and how bullying takes place. Before the smartphone age, bullying used to happen on the playground, during recess, in bathrooms, or while students were waiting for the bus. Now, it can occur anywhere. About 59% of U.S. teens have experienced on a personal level at least six types of online behaviors that are abusive, according to a new Pew Research Center survey.[12]

The six types of bullying are:

- Offensive name-calling
- Spreading false rumors about people
- Receiving unsolicited explicit images
- Constant surveillance by someone other than a parent as well as asking questions regarding location
- Making physical threats
- Leaking or sharing explicit images without their consent.

The most common type of harassment reported by the youth today is offensive name-calling, be it online or in real life. This type of abuse is often doled out by strangers (and even acquaintances) on the internet, and sometimes friends and even family in real life.

---

[12] Monica Anderson, September 2018, A Majority of Teens Have Experienced Some Form of Cyberbullying:
https://www.pewresearch.org/internet/2018/09/27/a-majority-of-teens-have-experienced-some-form-of-cyberbullying/#fn-21353-1

According to the report, 42% of teens have reported being called offensive names, either online or via text messages. In addition, about 32% of teens in the report stated that they were the victims of cyber abuse. A considerably smaller percentage of teens had been asked by other than a parent repeatedly about where they were at any given moment, who they were with or what they were doing. And 16% of teens had been receiving physical threats online according to the report.

The rate at which bullying was done more or less remained stagnant and the same in recent years. Also, about a fifth of students in a high school report that they were bullied while on the school property in the past year. Cyberbullying instances were experienced by these kids via social media, texts, or other digital means. What were the more likely to be bullied? Younger students and girls, as well as students who identified as a non-acceptable or normal gender, i.e., those who identified as lesbian, gay or bisexual, were the common targets in both cases.[13]

---

[13]https://nccd.cdc.gov/youthonline/App/questionsorlocations.aspx?Categoryid=C01

Gangs

Only 10.7% of students reported the presence of gangs in their schools, according to a report on school safety published by the U.S. Departments of Justice and Education.[14]Students in urban schools, including students from the Black and Hispanic communities, reported untoward activity by gangs at their school, more than the rest of the demographics.

Many students often join these gangs, whether they operate within or outside the school. What are the factors that draw children, teens, and young adults (especially girls) to this life when in school? One reason why young people join gangs (sometimes while in school and at other times after leaving/dropping out) is due to the need for belonging, self-esteem, and protection. These are the same feelings that come from being a member of a family. Youths, especially Blacks and Hispanics, are mostly drawn into gang activities because they don't have the back and support from guardians or parents, teachers, or community members

---

[14]Anlan Zhang, Ke Wang, Jizhi Zhang, Jana Kemp, Melissa Diliberti, March 2018, Indicators of School Crime and Safety: 2017: https://www.bjs.gov/content/pub/pdf/iscs17.pdf

– which they don't receive at all during their youth. They also often feel that nobody has their back and often feel misunderstood and alone. Who are the most likely to join gangs during or after school? Youth who are unsupervised, having access to only a few after-school activities or opportunities – which doesn't help them develop hobbies or make it easier to play sports.[15]

Poverty

Many don't realize how badly affected children living below the poverty line are, even in a rich nation such as America. The childhood poverty rate is much higher when compared to other developed countries. How?

In 2014, the poverty line recognized by the federal government in America for a family of four (2 adults and 2 children) was about $24,000. Additionally, a family must have income or must be able to earn twice the amount above to have a basic level of financial

---

[15]Randall G. Shelden, Sharon K. Tracy, and William B. Brown, 2013, Youth Gangs in American Society: https://youthtoday.org/2014/12/youth-gangs-in-american-society/

security, according to the U.S. Census Bureau.[16] Moreover, one in five children or youth in the U.S. lives in poverty. This means about 15.5 million impoverished kids are living in the U.S. A report was published in the Urban Institute, which states the percentage of American kids who spend at least a year in poverty before their 18th birthday, is 40%.[17] Only 10% of the National Budget is spent on kids for their education and other necessary components by the federal government. This is only a fraction of what is spent by other developed countries for their kids and youth.[18]

Homelessness

Homelessness is an epidemic ruling our streets. It

---

[16]Carmen DeNavas-Walt and Bernadette D. Proctor, September 2015, Income and Poverty in the United States: 2014:https://www.census.gov/content/dam/Census/library/publications/2015/demo/p60-252.pdf

[17]Caroline Ratcliffe, September 2015, Child Poverty and Adult Success: https://www.urban.org/sites/default/files/publication/65766/2000369-Child-Poverty-and-Adult-Success.pdf

[18]Julia Isaacs, Sara Edelstein, Heather Hahn, Ellen Steele, C. Eugene Steuerle, 2015, Report On Federal Expenditures On Children in 2014 and Future Projections: https://www.urban.org/sites/default/files/publication/71431/2000422-Kids-Share-2015-Report-on-Federal-Expenditures-on-Children-Through-2014.pdf

is estimated that about 3.5 million (or one in ten) young adults in the United States between the ages of 18 and 25 experience homelessness in a given year.[19] The homeless youth are vulnerable and feel disconnected from the rest of the world, which makes them more susceptible to joining the wrong crowd. Many of the homeless young adults have no choice but to live either in the homes of friends or relatives AND still don't have a fixed place to stay for an indefinite period. Others have no choice but to sleep in their cars, shelters, or on the streets.

Based on these statistics, one can safely say teachers and substitutes in the public education system have a lot of moral and social responsibility when it comes to addressing and eradicating the issues faced by youth. A lot of work needs to be done to effectively bridge the gap in social inequality in education. But we must never forget who is at the front lines of these issues: substitutes and teachers.

---

[19]Missed Opportunities: Youth Homelessness in America: https://www.chapinhall.org/wp-content/uploads/chapinhall_voyc_nationalreport_Final.pdf

Chapter 2
Overworked Substitutes and Teacher Recognition

"Teaching is a calling too. And I have always thought that teachers in their way are holy – angels leading their flock out of the darkness."

–*Jeanette Walls*

We have always looked at our school system to at least try to be a pillar or a shade for many of the issues mentioned in the previous chapter. However, unfortunately, policymakers have always resorted to filling teaching vacancies in public schools by lowering the standards of hiring (so that people with little or no preparation for teaching can be hired).[20]This is mostly done in areas or public schools of minority or low-income students. This means such schools, and the teachers teaching students who attend

---

[20]Joseph De Avila and Tawnell D. Hobbs, September 2017, Teacher Shortage Prompts Some States to Lower the Bar: https://www.wsj.com/articles/teacher-shortage-prompts-some-states-to-lower-the-bar-1504699200

are already overwhelmed by lack of funds and a lot of work. The reasoning given for this practice is that it's presumed that anyone can figure out how to teach. In fact, teachers that are fully prepared and certified – those who know the subject matter as well as (knowledge) of teaching and learning – are rated highly in their qualifications and very successful with students, as compared to teachers who teach without full preparation. Despite the lack of funding and resources, public school teachers, especially substitute teachers, give their all when it comes to teaching children and trying to make a difference.

Being a substitute teacher is difficult because substitutes rarely receive the respect they deserve, even if they're considered valuable to the classroom. A substitute teacher also is highly expendable and is meant to be moved wherever needed. As a result, they don't get much face time with the same classes to develop the rapport necessary to be effective with students. On the other hand, substitute teachers often don't take a lot of flak from the kids and aren't there to do anything but their jobs. Substitute teachers won't ask for a pay raise because their job is temporary, and they try harder because they know the position is constantly on the line. Anyone, even someone less experienced, can swoop in and take the job. This doesn't mean substitute teachers aren't hardworking and don't care about their students' well-being, education, and overall development. Yet, even if they serve an essential role in the education system and go above and beyond the call of duty, substitute teachers are often underappreciated and sometimes ignored. What are the issues that a substitute teacher faces?

Emergency, such as the usual class teacher taking a sudden leave of absence, can leave substitutes without a lesson plan and not enough time to plan one. They might get a call at 5:30 a.m. and need to report at the school by 7 a.m. Students sometimes refuse to take the substitute teacher seriously. These are among the factors that make the job of a substitute teacher difficult.[21]

We need to remember that:

---

[21]Ruth C. Perkins, December 1959, Problems of the Substitute Teacher: https://journals.sagepub.com/doi/abs/10.1177/019263655904325115?journal Code=bulc

"Of all the hard jobs around, one of the hardest is being a good teacher."

–Maggie Gallagher

The truth cannot be denied. And what is the truth? Teachers work long hours, day in and day out. While some people might argue that teachers don't work as hard as people in other professions (just because they don't work nights, weekends, and holidays), the truth is entirely different. Teachers are off in the summer, yes, but teachers work hard during eight- to 10-hour workdays and also take home a great deal of students' work and assignments to grade. When do they make the lesson plans? Either at night, after spending a long day in school and/or on weekends, of course.

During the summer, teachers attend professional development opportunities and do a lot of planning so they will be fully prepared for the next school year. Yes, even substitute teachers do that! This shows that substitute teachers are as important to the public education system as regular teachers. Those who attended a public school will most certainly vouch that some substitute teachers were more relaxed and flexible than the regular teacher. Yet, substitutes also can be strict, just like the regular class teacher but with lesser status. It doesn't make sense that such an important part of a typical school year's fabric (at least for the students) is treated poorly by the rest of the school system. For substitute teachers, their place in their school is more confusing to place and figure out. In fact, many have no option but to look after themselves and figure out lesson plans themselves with little preparation or support. This is one of the main reasons why there will be a difference in experience between a regular class teacher and a substitute teacher.

Important factors behind inequality and mistreatment of substitute teachers by the society at large are the school's policy as well as how students and parents deal with a substitute teacher. Let's see how badly this affects substitute teachers in numbers. There were about 587,240 substitute teachers who worked for annual standard pay of not even $32,360 but under as of spring 2018.[22] Many are paid hourly, with the mean falling at around $15.56 per hour. Are they given any benefits? In terms of perks of the job, a

---

[22]https://www.bls.gov/oes/current/oes253098.htm

substitute can sometimes enjoy a retirement fund. However, health insurance isn't offered. This inequality is defended by people due to a misconception. Some believe that substitute teachers aren't as qualified as regular teachers and don't deserve higher pay and benefits.

The basic qualifications that are required for substitute teachers to have are varied by state and district, as is the case with many professions. Some just require a high school diploma, while for others, substitute teaching candidates must have a bachelor's degree and some level of training to register. None have specific teaching experience requirements to be qualified for the job. Perhaps it's this inconsistency that leads to the misconceptions about substitute teachers, especially in public schools.

When it comes to subbing experience, according to the National Substitute Teachers Alliance, every question that concerns substitute teachers has 'it depends' as an answer. To summarize, we can see that the teaching aspect is the least difficult part of the profession, whether the teaching is done by the substitute teacher or the regular class teacher.

Teachers are Dedicated Professionals

"The best teachers teach from the heart, not from the book."

-Unknown

Though the origin of this quote is unknown, it cannot be truer today. It is very difficult to find a profession as dedicated as teachers are to their students and education. Here's a fact: during the 2017-2018 academic year, the average salary for a public school teacher nationwide was $60,483.[23] And the average pay for a substitute teacher was $80 a day before taxes.

This proves teachers often do whatever they have to do to meet the needs of the students, despite being paid less than other professions. In a nutshell, teachers are the cheerleaders of our youth, a voice, and advocates in schools. Teaching is not a job that ends when the school bell rings. It is a profession that goes home with them.

---

[23] Andy Kiersz and Marissa Perino, August 2019, Here's how much every US state pays its teachers and spends on a single student: https://www.businessinsider.com/teacher-salary-in-every-state-2018-4

Teachers Teach Against All Odds

"True teachers use themselves as bridges over which
they invite their students to cross; then, having
facilitated their crossing joyfully collapse,
encouraging them to create bridges of their own."
–Nikos Kazantzakis.

Teachers teach despite the challenges they face in the education sector, including lack of funding, budget cuts, large class sizes, few resources, lack of support, poor administration, testing demands, socio-economic challenges, little or no professional development, and the list goes on and on. Teachers teach despite these challenges and are proactive in finding solutions to them. Teachers will be the first to go into their pockets to buy classroom supplies for their students, buy lunch for a student in need, or stay after school to tutor a student who needs help.

So be sure to thank a teacher in your life. Remember, teachers not only teach students but teach all other professions. That makes teachers pretty darn important, like superheroes. If you can, shake a teacher's hand, write a handwritten letter, or take the time to talk with them. Money cannot buy extending your appreciation to a teacher.

"A teacher is never a giver of truth – he is a guide, a pointer to the truth that each student must find for himself. A good teacher is merely a catalyst." – Bruce Lee.

Because of this belief, substitutes and teachers are a catalyst that must be appreciated.

Chapter 3
Teachers

"If you have to put someone on a pedestal, put teachers. They are society's heroes."

–Guy Kawasaki

When I was a student, I had thoughts and perceptions about teachers that seemed pretty reasonable to my young mind. Back then, I was blown away by the fact that teachers HAD a life outside of school! Just imagine the shock and surprise after I figured out that my teachers didn't actually live in school... they just spent a lot of time there. In fact, seeing a teacher at a mall or someplace else, was very similar to seeing an extraterrestrial or an animal outside of its habitat or something very strange and bizarre. It just didn't make sense to me at that time.

After finishing school, I entered adulthood and 'real' life. This was the time when I thought I *really* knew about the teachers and the work they did. Then I thought I *really* knew about teachers. I mean, I had gone to school and conversed with them on this topic. I saw what their job was like daily, and knew the amount of work they put in for each student. The only thing I didn't know about the teaching experience was what it actually felt like to be a teacher in an American public school. This was until I became a substitute teacher.

After a few years of teaching, I must say, I realized I had it all wrong. In fact, everybody has it wrong. Everyone who is NOT a teacher can never know what a day is like in the life of a teacher. There are many incorrect perceptions of teachers out there.

Teachers Know Everything

This is what I thought when I was a kid. This is what the parents and the students think as well. I mean all teachers have to do is *teaching,* right? This is what they are paid to do, so it goes without a saying that teachers would know everything. The reason they became teachers is that they are subject matter experts and are, essentially, leaders.

But the reality is different. We treat teachers as AI robots or live versions of Google who know everything, but they don't. . . they are humans. In fact, only half of the teachers are usually only a little bit ahead of students on the topic they are teaching. This doesn't mean they don't know or don't find out, the reason teachers are always overworked is that they are constantly researching and studying various topics in their own subject area. I don't remember any incident in which I asked my teacher a question and got back an "I don't know" as the answer.

A Teacher's Job is to Teach

Sadly, a lot of people think like this... when, in reality, a teacher's job encompasses more than just teaching. And yet anytime issues with teaching and education come up in the news, anytime teachers complain or voice their concerns, radio talk shows feature citizen complaints, hurling remarks at the teachers that always come down to:

"What are they complaining about? They have the summers off, school ends at three, and all they have to do is teach." Well, that is far from true. The fact of the matter is teachers wear many hats. A teacher sometimes acts as a counselor, officer, coach, and even a friend. A teacher mentors students, motivates them, helps the ones who are struggling, and still finds the time to come up with new and exciting ways of engaging the students.

Teaching is Only an 8:30 to 3:30 Job

Just think about this for a second: your child receives his or her checked essay a few days after completing it by the teacher. On the page, there are various annotations, an overall comment at the bottom of the essay, and feedback, as well as an overall grade. Your child isn't the only student in that classroom, so the same must have been done for the other students.

Now consider; most classrooms consist of 30 students! Just when did the teacher read, comment on, and grade an accumulated total of 150 pages of students' work? This is just one example of the incredible amount of time teachers give to their work. So, how does the typical teacher spend time after school ends and all the students go home? Many teachers stay late in school, well after all the students leave.

Teachers spend nights and weekends grading work, responding to parents' emails and preparing lessons for their next classes. Here's the sad part: they only get paid until 3:30 p.m., because there is no concept of working while getting paid overtime. However, the job teachers must do to successfully run a class never ends that early in the afternoon. *"But, they are paid more!"* Considering how much time teachers put into their classes, they never actually get paid enough. However, we'll discuss more on that later. It's simple... being a teacher isn't easy, and no one should say or pretend that it is easy. Whether they are working in primary, secondary, or higher education, it doesn't matter – the job is demanding. Their jobs don't merely include giving quizzes to the students, giving homework and filling out worksheets. It is not simply a question of passing on knowledge to the students.

A teacher must (and does) keep so many other things in mind when teaching, such as providing lessons in discipline, ensuring engagement, fostering empathy, mentoring the students, and looking after students' needs. A really good teacher will inspire his or her class, even students striving to be the best. A teacher's most important job is to MAKE young people want to learn[24] (and they do!) and to appreciate the importance of knowledge and education. So, it doesn't matter how many laptops there are in a

---

[24]Thea Peetsma, Peter Sleegers, Eric E.J. Thoonen, & Frans J. Oort, July 2011, Can Teachers Motivate Students to Learn: https://www.researchgate.net/publication/233172166_Can_teachers_motivate_students_to_learn

classroom. It isn't important how many posters line the walls or what type of clothing is permitted in schools. What matters most to students and their education are the teachers; that is the undeniable truth.

Students know better than anyone the power wielded by a good teacher, but the public and to a degree, boards of education, fail to understand how this one, simple and fallible resource could be so vital when it comes to producing smart, successful citizens. Yet, even after countless studies, the results remain the same: We need teachers, now and forevermore! Here's why:

Every teacher doesn't teach just content from textbooks and PowerPoint presentation slides, but also teach their students a wide range of skills they need to be more successful as adults. A study[25] published in the Journal of Political Economy shows just how important it is to foster those skills. Teachers who help students improve non-cognitive skills help to raise their grades. This helps increase the likelihood of

---

[25]C.Kirabo Jackson, August 2018, What Do Test Scores Miss? The Importance of Teacher Effects on Non-Test Score Outcomes: https://www.journals.uchicago.edu/doi/abs/10.1086/699018?Journalcode=jpe&

graduating from high school. To support this, the author of the study, C. Kirabo Jackson, looked at and studied data of over 570,000 students studying in different schools in North Carolina. It was found that ninth-grade teachers had a significant impact on those students who improved their non-cognitive skills with the help of their teachers. How?

In addition, these students were also more likely to have higher attendance and grades, as well as more likely to graduate than their peers. Even then, teachers have to face a number of challenges on a day-to-day basis, many of which also indirectly impact their students negatively.

Challenges

There's a before and an after picture when it comes to the treatment of teachers. Let's look at the "before" picture first. In the novel "East of Eden," John Steinbeck writes:

"In the country, the repository of art and science was the school, and the schoolteacher shielded and carried the torch of learning and beauty ... The teacher was not only an intellectual paragon and a social leader but also a matrimonial catch of the countryside. A family could indeed walk proudly if a son married

the schoolteacher."

The above is something that cannot come in the America of today, a country where teachers are five times more likely to work at a second job[26] than the average full-time worker. Moreover, the costs of living rise with every passing year, which makes it difficult for teachers to survive with low pay. An economist at the Institute for Research on Labor and Employment at the University of California, Berkeley, rightly says:

"That's a really bad situation to be in, being asked to pay more as your pay is actually declining. In real terms, meaning after you adjust for inflation, the average U.S. teacher today makes $30 less a week than they used to."

Constant pay for teachers has decreased by as much as 15%, according to the National Education Association.[27] Another report by The Economist[28] states that teachers earn only 60% as much as a

---

[26] Alexia Fernandez Campbell, April 2018, More Teachers Are Working Part-Time Jobs to Pay the Bills: https://www.vox.com/policy-and-politics/2018/4/4/17164718/teachers-work-part-time-jobs
[27] Jenny Abamu, April 2018, The Data Tells All: Teacher Salaries Have Been Declining For Years: https://www.edsurge.com/news/2018-04-05-the-data-tells-all-teacher-salaries-have-been-declining-for-years
[28] May 2018, Behind the teacher strikes that have roiled five states:https://www.economist.com/united-states/2018/05/05/behind-the-teacher-strikes-that-have-roiled-five-states

professional with a similar level of education. What is the average salary for a teacher? In many states, it is under $50,000. With low wages, stretched resources, and twice the amount of workforce, American educators are more likely to burnout and quit the profession, according to Linda Hammond, President, and CEO of the Learning Policy Institute[29]. Additionally, there is a massive teacher shortage in America since less than 35% have studied to become teachers in recent years, which forces schools in the nation to hire more than 100,000 people who don't even have the proper experience and qualifications.

As an article in the New York Times reports[30], many school districts across different states have begun to recruit instructors from low-wage countries because of the shortage of qualified teachers as well as the inability to hire them at lower pay. However, low wages aren't the only issue that teachers face under the current education system. In the golden age of education, the federal government provided easy

---

[29]https://edition.cnn.com/2018/04/27/opinions/teacher-strikes-more-than-pay-darling-hammond-opinion/index.html

[30] Dana Goldstein, May 2018, Teacher Pay Is So Low in Some U.S. School Districts That They're Recruiting Overseas:https://www.nytimes.com/2018/05/02/us/arizona-teachers-philippines.html

access to ample resources that teachers could use in the classroom, went to seminars to develop skills, and received a sense of fulfillment as a direct result. Today, teachers have little time or money to do any of this. They are overworked and underpaid; even then, many teachers pay off their own pockets to pay for classroom supplies. According to a survey of public teachers, 94% pay (an average of) $479 a year[31] for classroom supplies out of their own wallets. They do this even when knowing there is little to no chance of reimbursement.

In the end, it's not even about the money. Teaching was never a profession that people chose to become rich. In fact, those who choose to teach do so due to the love for children and the need to give something back... they even once enjoyed the respect and status shown in Steinbeck's quote. According to the head of the education division at the Organization for Economic Cooperation and Development has come up with observations after spending years conducting

---

[31] Maria Danilova, May 2018, Study: Despite modest income, nearly all teachers pay for class needs out of own pocket:
https://www.usatoday.com/story/money/personalfinance/2018/05/15/nearly-all-teachers-spend-own-money-school-needs-study/610542002/

careful international comparisons and analysis on education. What is the verdict? The countries that hire top-level college graduates as teachers actually perform the best in public education, because they pay reasonably well and invest a lot in their professional development. Additionally, the society and its people of those countries show deep respect for the teaching profession.

On the other hand, in the United States, what do we do when we meet a member of the armed services? We thank them for their service. So why don't we do the same when meeting a teacher? When was the last time you did the same for a public school teacher?

The Many Faces of the Teacher – Roles They Play[32]

"Teachers are unparalleled in the role they play in children's lives."

–Jon Porter

Simply spending more money doesn't always guarantee the best results, yet, some studies suggest

---

[32]Erlita A. Gulane, The Many Faces of a Teacher:
http://local.lsu.edu.ph/institutional_research_office/publications/vol.15no.7/2.html

that there's a link between a teacher's pay and the students' achievements. The education bureaucracy in America is rigid, but the central problem is something else. Being a teacher in America has become a thankless job. Yet it is one profession that makes all others possible. What are the many different roles a teacher plays in his or her lifetime? If we think about it, the traditional role of the teacher in the school is a **provider of information.** This is the most basic role played by a teacher.

The **surrogate parent** is the second role that a teacher plays. Why is this role important? Many students don't have the parental contact necessary for them to develop and reach their full potential. In fact, there are some kids whose parents work long hours and don't even have time to spend together after coming back. Others come from broken families, households run by single parents, or abusive families. Whatever the reason, those parents are largely absent from their children's lives. These children have no one else but the teacher for support and advice in matters of life and education. This is a very important and responsible job.

The third and very important role a teacher plays is that of a **counselor.** Today, students struggle through many external issues that affect performance at school. Some students require special education or classes due to certain needs. The emotional needs of children who attend school from broken or destitute families also largely go unmet and unnoticed. As mentioned above, many live in single-parent homes where their mother or father must work fulltime and also play the role of the good/bad cop.

This often leaves kids with deep emotional deficits that not only prevent them from paying attention in class but also influence much of the negative decision-making. A teacher can lend an ear to the student. Sometimes, a heartfelt word of encouragement and advice can make a world of difference. The sub-roles a teacher plays for their students is that of a **friend** and **mentor.** Years of experience in the field provides teachers with enough know-how of different matters. A good teacher is trusted by his or her students, and they know they'll receive good advice when it comes to school and academics. A good teacher also will be ready to mentor children struggling in any way, either in school or outside. Teachers teach against all the odds and despite the challenges prevalent in education, such as lack of funds, budget cuts, large class sizes, lack of or few resources, lack of support, poor administration, testing demands, various socio-economic challenges, few or no professional development opportunities, and the list goes on and on. Teachers teach despite all these challenges. The least that we can do is thank and appreciate them. Remember, teachers aren't merely teaching students; they are preparing the next batch of all professions. That makes them pretty darn important, like a superhero! How to appreciate them? A simple "thank you" can suffice but if you wish to do a little extra, you can:

Write a Handwritten Letter –It means a lot to receive a handwritten letter, especially in today's digitalized culture. Receiving a well-thought and written letter from a student or parent shows to teachers that they are important enough to warrant a little extra effort and though. Nothing else will show to your child's teacher that he or she is appreciated for their hard work and dedication. You can add in something a little extra to the handwritten note, like fresh baked goods, and have your child bring them in the class. The treat may be just what the teacher needs to get through a tough week. More than tangible gifts are intangible ones. The best gift of appreciation a parent or a child can offer to a teacher is the gift of respect, which makes sense considering the teacher-blaming climate of our schools. No one but the public can help create respect and a chain of appreciation towards the teacher. Where do we start? Simply by viewing the teacher and this profession as noble and needed, as well as important.

"Teaching is not a lost art, but the regard for it is a lost tradition."

-Jacques Barzun

Chapter 4
Leadership & the
Administration

"Teachers make a difference in the classroom, but it's the Principle who makes a difference in the school."

-Anon

Have you considered just how many people work behind the scenes at a typical public high school? There are plenty of valid reasons why the most recognizable employees within a school district are the teachers, yet, they aren't the only ones in the school personnel who has the best interests of the child at heart. Even before the teachers, the administration and support staff hold the fort at public schools for all the students enrolled.[33]It's a simple fact: Without leadership, a ship cannot run. For teachers, the job of providing structure and discipline to the students

---

[33]Cynthia S. Johnson, October 2011, School Administrators and the Importance of Utilizing Action Research: http://www.ijhssnet.com/journals/Vol_1_No_14_October_2011/11.pdf

begins with the Principal's leadership skills. We must recognize how critical this is. I can remember when the Principal was out for a few days covering for another Principal in the district. Most people think that because Principals are not in the classrooms, they are not as effective as teachers. But this is far from the truth. When the Principal is out for a few days, we see more students engaging in behavioral issues in the halls and not listening to teachers' directions.

Principals deal with mostly negative issues in our schools in addition to trying to implement standards set by the state. This is a highly stressful job that also falls on the assistant Principals. For people to undertake this role, they need to have professional excellence and a heart of gold. They decide to serve our public schools in a way that is arguably much more challenging than a teacher's job or even being a teacher. School personnel can be divided into three distinct categories. What are the roles and responsibilities of these people?

School Leaders

This group of people is responsible for developing educational policies for their school. They also make sure the school can support and implement those policies by ensuring that they have the resources. Highlighted below, from the order of importance within the public school hierarchy are:

Board of Education

It is the board of education that makes decisions regarding education in a particular state. Five elected community members comprise the board of education. The eligibility requirement for a board member, i.e., who can serve, varies by state-to-state. This group of people generally meets once a month to discuss matters of importance and set school policy when needed. The district superintendent is hired by the board. Moreover, the board also considers the recommendations given by the superintendent when deciding policy or resource/fund allocation. In fact, any decision that concerns the operation of the district, the board consults with the superintendent.

Superintendent

The superintendent is hired by the board of education and looks after the day-to-day operations and tasks of the school district. This means each school district has a different superintendent, who also provides suggestions and ideas to the board in a variety of areas. However, the main responsibility is handling the financial matters of the school district. Superintendents also work side-by-side with the state government.

Assistant Superintendent

It's difficult to take care of education and school matters in a large district, which is where the assistant superintendent enters the picture. The job of this professional is to look after one or several assigned parts of the daily operations for his or her district. The assistant superintendents report to the district superintendent.

Principal

The Principal's job is to look after the daily operations that happen in an individual school building within a district. This means the Principal is charged with ensuring students and faculty/staff in that building's welfare – catering to their needs and handling any issues that may crop up on any given day.

A large school district also has assistant Principals, who work under the Principals of their school. The assistant Principal may oversee a specific part or parts of a school's daily operations.

School Support Staff

In addition to the administration, the school support staff also plays a huge role in the education and betterment of the child.

The people of note in the school support staff are:

Administrative Assistant

An important position, a school administrative assistant, is required to know the day-to-day school operations as well as anyone. He/she also communicates most often with the parents of the students. A good administrative assistant also screens makes the administrator's job much easier by taking calls and making appointments, answering emails of parents queries, and supervising on matters of lesser importance.

School Nutritionist

A well-balanced diet is important for children who require nutrients and energy to perform well in school. A school nutritionist is the one who is responsible for creating a menu for the school lunch that meets state nutrition standards, which must be met for all meals served at school. In addition, nutritionists are responsible for ordering the food that will be served, ensuring fresh ingredients are used. They also collect and keep track of all the money taken in and spent by the school's nutrition program. A school nutritionist is also responsible for monitoring the students who are eating the school-provided lunches and determine which students qualify for free/reduced lunches.

School Nurse

Accidents and injuries can happen in a school setting. A school nurse is on duty in the case of accidents at school and provides general first aid. A school nurse, depending on the curriculum requirements, can also teach students about health and health-related issues.

These examples illustrate how each member of the administration and staff is important to the seamless operation of a school. It is safe to say these staff members are the backbone of the education sector as no school can operate effectively without them lending support to the teachers, students, and parents.

Misconceptions about the School Administration

There are no ifs, and, or buts in this matter. Without these essential roles, our public school system wouldn't operate effectively or efficiently. These professionals are the ones who determine education delivery throughout school districts and requirements for future development and progress.

In addition, school administrators support the teaching staff so that the education facility can operate at an efficient and smooth pace. Yet a school's administration isn't thought of as important when it comes to delivering quality educational services. However, one thing is for sure, without this department and the service provided, an entire campus is at risk of inefficient operation.

Lastly, but more importantly, the administrative roles that provide students with a safe and secure space in which they can learn, should not be ignored. In the end, the bottom line of every school administrator is to provide a safe and studies-conducive environment to the students, who are healthy and capable of learning, both emotionally and physically.

And yet, there are so many misperceptions about the administration of a school, even more so than the teachers. The school administration world faces its own set of stereotypes that are not even correct. So, what are some of the common misconceptions faced by administrators in education?

They're Paid Too Much[34]

Let's be honest. Nobody goes into education or school administration thinking, *"Here's where I'll make the big bucks."* And that applies to everyone who works in the public school system, from the school Principal to superintendents of some of the largest districts in the nation.

In regard to how much each person working within the public school system earns, I want to say that everyone in education is usually paid far below what is deserved.

Additionally, many who assume they (the teachers) are paid more actually compare the number with a teacher's salary to other professions that require similar training. In order to make an accurate

---

assumption, the salary of people working in admin should be raised to the same levels as other professions that require the same qualifications.

They Have Little Idea What It's Like to Teach

There is a misconception that administrators are disconnected from the classroom. People who believe this forget that many administrators were teachers who had the opportunity to take a little more control of the helm and go into administration.

People can't really use this as the "Us versus Them" mentality in twenty-first-century schools. If everyone isn't working together, the school will fail. Administrators are well-aware of what is happening inside the classroom. In fact, many administrator education programs now have training that requires prospective Principals or superintendents to work closely with teachers on developing projects, curriculum, or finding solutions to assessments and data issues.

Administrators Don't Provide Flexibility to Teachers

There is another misperception about a school's administration – that they don't provide flexibility to teachers or allow them to take risks. It makes sense to be hesitant when it comes to bringing massive change to how things are run, but like teachers and parents, administrators want nothing more than for students to continue learning and to succeed.

This isn't an issue that concerns power over teachers. Rather, it is an issue of accountability. In the end, administrators have to ensure that only the best decisions are made for a district or school while keeping the policies and compliance issues in mind.

All Administrators are Ladder Climbers

A gross misperception that maligns school administrators is that they are all like politicians, and all that these hardworking people think about is climbing the ladder. Being devoted to a career path sometimes means you have to go further into it. This is not ladder climbing, and no, administrators don't "step onto little people" to get there. Another misconception is that administrators have power, and it goes to their heads. The truth is they don't have any more power than teachers. Yes, they make decisions sometimes that impact the school and district, but that power comes from the board of education. It comes from the community; and from being a team member.

Twenty-first-century administrators are dealing with issues and challenges that are more complex than trying to convince parents to send their children to school – as was the case in the days of old.[35]

There are unique challenges faced by school administrators today that are above ensuring good attendance and grades of students. Below are some of the more salient issues that school administrators face today:

Making Strategic Decisions – The school administration sits right at the center of managing and controlling the school body and its activities. Hence, school administrators are responsible for looking after and ensuring discipline, making schedules, and managing staff, among other things. This requires

---

[35]J.L. Cornelius & Joe P. Cornelius, The Challenges of Public School Administrators in the New Millennium:
http://www.nationalforum.com/Electronic%20Journal%20Volumes/Corneli us,%20J.%20L.%20The%20Challenges%20of%20Public%20School%20Admin istrators%20In%20The%20New%20Millennium.pdf

taking strategic decisions that consider the best of the school and its students while delivering results.

Recruit Capable Staff – Recruiting capable and qualified teachers to teach students is a very important issue, and a challenge considering finding good teachers can be difficult to find due to immense competition.

Maintaining Student Discipline – Students today face a lot of their issues every day, which deters many from focusing on studies and school. Some of the students are involved in gangs or drugs, and many have to juggle after-school jobs with a volatile life at home.

Staff Retention – The latest trend in the field of education is moving toward smaller size classes. However, there is trouble retaining good and competent teachers. In fact, school administrators are struggling to find capable teachers to tutor the next generation of children.

Despite the above challenges faced by administrators (and there are many more), schools and children are given top priority. In the end, a successful school is about more than just teaching. While good teaching and learning are crucial, it's the administration that provides a well-rounded operation and coverage of seamless operations, encompassing the whole child. Effective administration and operations support an education that goes well beyond imparting knowledge.

School operations teams ensure that the daily needs of students are met, that they receive healthy and nutritious meals, and learn in a safe environment. Beyond day-to-day tasks, the administrative team is often responsible for recording, checking, and analyzing student data, so they can enable teachers to tailor their approach to the needs of each student, respectively.

These are all the reasons we need to give more importance to the role school administrators fill and appreciate these individuals for their hard work and a job well done. We need to understand that a school administrator does all the best he or she is able to, given the resources at disposal and the circumstances in which the school finds itself. We need to walk in their shoes, as Lee Harper says in "To Kill a Mockingbird":

"You never really know a man until you understand things from his point of view until you climb into his skin and walk around it."

Chapter 5
Substitute Teachers

"We need to reward the 'thankless job' of substitute teaching with better pay and chances for permanent positions. I look forward to the day when no student comes home saying, 'I didn't learn much today... we had a sub.' "

–AdoraSvitak

Substitute teachers don't get the credit they rightfully deserve. They often have the same level of college training as certified teachers, and yet are treated as expendable by the public. Who steps up and teaches a roomful of children, ensuring that classroom instruction continues when *regular* teachers are unable to come to school – often at the last minute? In many places across the nation, substitute teachers are asked to shoulder a significant amount of responsibility, especially if they are long-term substitutes.

Additionally, they are required to have an undergraduate degree, as well as being encouraged to work toward obtaining teacher certification. What does this tell us? The work substitute teachers do IS IMPORTANT. Even then, the world has some misgivings and misperceptions about subs, which is one reason why nobody treats these noble individuals the same way as regular teachers.

Misperceptions about Substitute Teachers

Substitute teachers are also professional educators. So yes, they should be considered as more than "babysitters" by the parents, children, and even the school administration. Why? Well, for one thing, it's extremely disrespectful toward these professionals. Most substitute teachers also have other fulltime jobs or careers besides this.

One should not assume these hardworking individuals don't have professional lives outside the classroom where they use a lot of energy after pouring their hearts and soul into the classroom. Yes, despite the common misperception that a substitute teacher has little interest in actually teaching, many enter this profession because of their love for children and want to make a difference. Most substitute teachers could become certified teachers. However, their work outside of the classroom doesn't allow for a full-time job. In a world where substitute teachers are already viewed as individuals who don't work as hard as regular teachers, students shouldn't think that having a sub in the classroom is an opportunity to abandon their responsibilities and respect for the teacher. They should work just as hard as they do when the regular teachers are in the classroom. We need to teach the importance of substitute teachers, especially in the absence of the regular teacher. It's because of the sub teacher that maternity leaves for regular teachers are possible. It's because of the sub teacher that even after emergency leaves, the classroom still operates.

Regular teachers also must help in any way they can, by making detailed lesson plans and leaving specific instructions for the substitute teacher. Contrary to popular belief, substitute teachers aren't placeholders – they contribute a lot of value to our children's future. They are the backup when the soldiers on your frontline are indisposed or cannot make it to the classroom. The least we can do for substitute teachers is to be good to them, considering the effort they put in and the hope they have for our children.

"But I looked over at him with his substitute math teacher glasses and hopeful expression, and my smile faded. He hadn't learned yet that things didn't work out just because you wanted them to."

–Morgan Matson.

Inconsistent Wage Woes of the Sub

The Bureau of Labor Statistics states subs nation-wide aren't paid the same. In Maryland, for example, subs are paid an hourly wage of $28.29, according to May 2018 BLS data. The highest-paying states are Hawaii, Oregon, and Vermont. Substitute teachers in Alabama earn the least, at just $9.19 an hour. The next in line to offer the lowest wages to sub teachers on average are Tennessee, Mississippi, and Idaho. Montgomery, Alabama, pays subs the lowest subs of all U.S. cities, at $8.33 an hour, whereas Springfield, Massachusetts, pays the highest at $26.84.[36]

Subs Get Called Early in the Morning

The early bird gets the worm in the substitute teacher world. Teachers are called into work about 5 a.m., as reported by the education site ThoughtCo. After getting and accepting the temporary position, subs may have to report to a different school than the one in which they most recently subbed. Usually, the

---

[36] https://www.bls.gov/home.htm

sub follows the lesson plan designed and left behind by the regular teacher, just before class starts. Many subs don't even have this. They often go in without any preparation or knowledge of the lesson plan. This is why they are forced to improvise as best as possible.

The U.S. is Experiencing a Shortage of Substitute Teachers

In the 2015-2016 school year, U.S. schools were short 64,000 teachers, according to the Learning Policy Institute,[37] Special education suffered the most teacher shortages, followed by a shortage in teachers teaching science, bilingual studies, and math. Schools in very poor areas and where students of color were in the majority also suffered the most from this shortage.

The situation has now become dire, rising to a level of concern that requires instant action. It's strange to note very little is being done, considering some states' heavy reliance on long-term substitute teachers. In fact, the state of Michigan uses long-term substitutes

---

[37]Tara Garcia Mathewson, April 2017, Subshortage leaves schools scrambling when teachers call in sick:https://hechingerreport.org/sub-shortage-leaves-schools-scrambling-when-teachers-call-in-sick/

more than any other in the country.[38] How essential are long-term substitute teachers? Well, many states are hiring full-time substitute teachers for many of the positions and subjects that are usually given to regular teachers

In the 2018-2019 class year, classrooms were led (and students taught) by 2,500 long-term substitute teachers. Why the dependence and reliance on substitute teachers? Because these professionals are only required to complete 90 semester hours of college credit and score a 2.0 grade-point average at a college in order to qualify for substitute teaching.

According to a 2016 report[39], Las Vegas— a state which has the most bottom-performing school districts in the U.S.[40] makes use of long-term substitute teachers (as well as regular ones) with lesser qualifications. As with every profession, this one also

---

[38]Mike Wilkinson, Ron French, August 2019, Michigan leans on long-term substitutes as its schools struggle: https://www.bridgemi.com/talent-education/michigan-leans-long-term-substitutes-its-schools-struggle
[39]Sarah Gonser, November 2016, Why Las Vegas Is Recruiting Uncertified Teachers: https://www.theatlantic.com/education/archive/2016/11/are-uncertified-teachers-better-than-substitutes/509099/
[40]Meghin Delaney, October 2017, Nevada list of underperforming schools includes 44 in Clark County:
https://www.reviewjournal.com/news/education/nevada-list-of-underperforming-schools-includes-44-in-clark-county/

comes with a lot of challenges and issues. While teachers don't get into this profession for the money, it's no secret that teachers are underpaid and overworked. What about substitute teachers? Do they fare any better than their regular counterparts? Not really.

How Much Do Substitute Teachers Make?

There are many factors to consider when it comes to deciding the wages of a substitute teacher (and yes, they aren't the same as a regular teacher's). Sub teachers can be expected to be paid by the day, whether they are teaching in an elementary, middle, or high school.

It also depends on the state, school district, the teacher's certification status, and whether they have a college degree. In fact, pay varies dramatically after considering all these factors, ranging anywhere from $20 to as much as $190 per day.[41] Do you see the problem? Sub teachers don't have a set pay range in public schools. Many districts offer monetary incentives in the form of daily pay increases or

---

[41]https://study.com/resources/substitute-teacher-salary

bonuses for substitutes who work more than a certain number of days in the school year. It's uncommon for a substitute teacher to receive additional benefits on top of their daily pay, which is why it's even more important for us to appreciate them for the warriors they are. The only way a substitute teacher can qualify for any type of benefit is if they join a substitute teacher union that provides the option of receiving health, vision, and dental insurance.

Getting a license and certification also impacts and increases pay.

Average Substitute Teacher Salary

What is the average pay substitute teacher? The national average annual salary for substitute teachers in elementary and secondary schools was $31,510 in 2017.[42] However, here's the thing; just as daily pay varies from state to state. Similarly, the average salary made by a substitute teacher can vary significantly among different regions or cities, even within a state. Additionally, the average daily pay rate of substitute

---

[42]https://study.com/resources/substitute-teacher-salary

teachers is only $75 or $80 per day. This is a very concerning amount, considering the current economy.

Substitute Teacher Salary by State

As mentioned above, the pay for substitute teachers varies significantly throughout the country, with the highest paying states offering close to $30,000 or more a year as compared to the lowest-paying states[43]. Below is a chart that features some of the average salaries substitute teachers made in 2017, from the highest to the lowest.

High Paying States	Average Annual Salary
New York	$31,037
Massachusetts	$30,747
New Hampshire	$29,941
Washington	$29,809
Hawaii	$29,393

---

[43]https://www.ziprecruiter.com/Salaries/What-Is-the-Average-Substitute-Teacher-Salary-by-State

Lowest Paying States	Average Salary
Michigan	$24,692
Mississippi	$24,305
Missouri	$24,239
Florida	$23,956
North Carolina	$21,744

Substitute Teacher Day-by-Day Hourly Salary[44]

Wages of a substitute teacher aren't typically determined using an hourly wage system. In fact, a majority of states pay sub teachers a daily rate or a half-day rate. How is the daily rate set? It's set by either the individual school districts or by the state's department of education. Estimated percentile of the wage earned in a day, on an hourly basis, is:

- Lowest 10% Hourly Pay: $9.04

---

[44]https://study.com/resources/substitute-teacher-salary

- Median Hourly Pay: $13.59

- Highest 10% Hourly Pay: $22.68

Long-Term Substitute Teacher Salary

Either the individual school districts or the states decide the specific requirements considered for determining a long-term substitute. Many states require a teacher to teach in the same position for about 20 or more consecutive school days. Only then can a substitute teacher receive a raise in daily pay, and, in some states, be given a first-year teacher's salary and benefits.

Permanent substitutes are hired to work every day of the school year in some districts. The duties and responsibilities of a permanent sub teacher vary today. These permanent substitutes are often given a higher daily pay rate and/or the same health benefits coverage provided to full-time employees. Keep in mind that these examples are distinct to specific areas and districts and that each district or state will have its own set of policies regarding paying long-term and permanent substitutes. It should also be remembered that even the highest pay a substitute teacher makes isn't the same amount as what a full-time teacher makes. I don't have any intention of pitting one against the other by pointing out this difference; regular full-time teachers face the same issues that substitutes do, yet, there are some additional issues and challenges that are only faced by the substitute teachers.

Challenges Faced By Substitute Teachers

Every substitute teaching job is different, which means the challenges they face aren't the same. Sometimes, a sub teacher is charged to look after a class while the kids watch a movie or complete an assignment left by their regular teacher. These are the so-called easy days. On other days, the teacher will follow a detailed lesson plan.

This is to ensure that the students' time isn't wasted, and they learn something worthwhile, according to the curriculum. A substitute teacher's workday lasts six to seven hours and only ends when the students go home. The first challenge sub teachers face is the uncertainty of what the duty will be on a particular day because they fill positions for only the period of time a regular full-time teacher cannot make it to class. This means the sub teacher might teach at an inner-city high school science class one day, teach third-graders at an international school two days, and then spend two months teaching junior high English at a private school. Yes, sub teachers have the freedom to choose which assignments to pursue at which schools, however, sometimes options are limited, and any job has to do to make money.

This also means that a sub teacher should know a little bit about every subject and be comfortable teaching various age groups and grades. Other challenges faced by substitute teachers are:

- Communicating adequately with the classroom teachers for whom they come as a replacement. Written lesson plans can be sparse or detailed, but often already have complex ideas which the sub might not know about. This can make teaching difficult.

- Having control over the classroom is another issue that most sub teachers have difficulty achieving. Many students have lost respect for the teacher due to a number of reasons — including behavior management issues. Moreover, the sub teachers are often at a disadvantage if the regular teacher hasn't prepared students for the eventual appearance of a sub teacher.

- Not receiving enough backup from school administrators when students are referred to the office for discipline problems. Even now, it's unclear whether sub teachers can dole out punishment to students.

- Being asked to work in special education classes, even if having little or no training beforehand and not receiving it from the school.

- Receiving respect of students, their parents, and school administrators, ensuring learning isn't interrupted during the absence of the regular teacher.

Additionally, sub teachers aren't fans of school holidays because they don't have a set salary and work one day at a time. This is one reason many of them face financial uncertainty, especially when holidays come into the picture. Imagine entire school districts have the entire Thanksgiving week off. For subs, this isn't a chance to relax as they depend on day-to-day work. For them, a quarter of their paycheck for that month is already gone by the time the week is over. It can be difficult when they also have to pay for student loans, insurance, and other expenses.

These are just some of the reasons substitute teachers need to be appreciated more by students, their parents, and the school administration. Did you know the third Friday in November was designated as the annual Substitute Educators Day, to honor subs around the country? The question is, though we have this day, do we do enough to extend our gratitude. Besides bringing awareness to the work substitute teachers do, the special day also supports subs in their quest for health benefits, professional development, and fair wages. Although most substitute teachers don't see the same kids day after day, they can have a meaningful impact on their students' lives. And they do! This was my favorite part of this job.

Chapter 6
Special Education
Teacher

"A good special education teacher is hard to find and even harder to hang on to."

−Lourdes Garcia-Navarro

Did you know classrooms in 2013 often taught special education students and general education students IN THE SAME CLASSROOM? Why? At that time, the national trend was in support of placing all children together in one classroom, even if some had disabilities. Back then, teachers didn't have the tools or training to teach special needs students or who might need special education.

So, what happened? Teachers could not call out a misbehaving child in front of the class if the student had a behavioral disability. There have been instances when children saw it as "an attack and disrespect issue." A period of time passed, then teachers figured out a way to navigate such situations without losing the respect of students. Over a period of time, the teachers figured out how to deal with such situations. They also learned ways to keep special needs students invested in the task, activity, or lesson by breaking down information to small and easy to learn chunks, which helped the struggling kids.

This strategy and many more were entirely self-taught. They were still required to have the necessary qualifications (at least a bachelor's degree and a teaching certificate), but no teacher was required by policy to take training on how to teach students with disabilities. Many teachers were forced to learn on the job through a lot of trial and error, which doubled their work and reduced attention to the general education kids.

Dire Need for Special Education Teachers

Teachers already have a lot on their plate, as highlighted in the previous chapters. They cannot be expected to wear an additional hat and teach special education kids, who require a different method of teaching. Additionally, there are an estimated 6.6 million special needs students in America today, making up nearly 13% of our public school population[45]. What makes us so sure that all teachers are fully equipped and qualified to handle special needs students? Not only handle them but also teach them in a way they can easily comprehend. Keep in mind that the majority of teachers don't even have the requisite certification needed to become a special education teacher or engage in regular training related to special education.

This is where teachers who have experience and prior knowledge of teaching special education students, enter the scene. What is the role and responsibility of special education teachers? They work with students who have shortcomings and disabilities, which can be physical, emotional, mental, and physical.

These teachers have to modify general educational lessons, which include reading, writing, and math as core subjects. In addition, they also have to make them fit and appropriate to learn for specially disabled students, ranging from mild to moderate disabilities.

---

[45] May 2018, Opportunities for Improving Programs and Services for Children with Disabilities:
https://www.ncbi.nlm.nih.gov/books/NBK518920/

In addition, basic skills are also taught by these teachers to students who have severe disabilities.

Duties of a Special Education Teacher

A teacher who trains in special education typically does the following:

When a child comes in the class on his or her first day, the special education teacher assesses the learning capabilities of the child. This helps to determine their needs, which makes it easier to develop teaching plans accordingly.

The next step they take is to adapt and modify lessons and tailor them as per the student's disability. Individualized Education Programs are developed for each student with the information collected in the first few days. A special education teacher also makes and implements activities according to what each student would prefer or like.

Additionally, the special education teacher acts as a supervisor and mentor to TAs or IAs who also have to work with students with disabilities.

A special education teacher also helps in the effective transitioning of the student from one grade to another, and sometimes even after graduation. Judging from the above, the work of a special education teacher is not limited to just one person, but instead, it's a cohesive effort of a team that comprises of general education teachers, counselors, school superintendents, and parents.

Some classrooms and resource centers only teach students with disabilities. What does the teacher do in this setting? The job of the teacher, in this case, is to design, modify, and then implement specially designed lessons – for each student. In addition, the teacher also typically teaches students in small groups or one-on-one.

However, the public school system doesn't believe in excluding kids with special needs, which is why students with disabilities attend classes with general education students in an inclusive classroom.

In such a setting, the classroom is headed by both the teachers — where the special education teacher spends most of his or her day assisting the special education kids. In what ways? They help present information learned in the classroom in a way that is more easily understandable for students with disabilities. In addition to their everyday duties and responsibilities, a special education teacher also collaborates with teacher assistants, psychologists, and social workers of an area of the school to understand and accommodate special requirements of students in a better manner. Some also help students who are struggling in specific subjects such as reading and math.

Special education teachers don't discriminate and prefer to teach one student instead of another. It's true, many prefer to teach students with a specific disability or special need (which they have studied and trained for), but in many cases, a special education teacher doesn't have a choice regarding the student he or she takes under their wing. Some teachers focus on children who are blind and deaf, and with physically impaired students.

Some of these teachers may also work with students who fall under the autism spectrum or have any emotional disorders such as depression and anxiety. Special education teachers are really important as they help students to develop the necessary basic life skills needed for survival. Students with moderate disabilities are taught the necessary skills to live independently and even find a job. Some parents and general education teachers say that special education teachers have easy jobs. They don't. Hard work and immense dedication are always displayed by special education teachers, yet even then, outsiders can still downplay and simply not understand the magnitude of their work.

What happens when the public, as well as the system (to an extent), downplays the importance of a special education teacher's work? This often leaves the teachers with a variety of social issues to tackle and conquer, issues that are sometimes not even recognized as such by the rest of us:

Dearth of Professional Development

One concern that isn't addressed by the public school system is that of professional development or a lack of it, within a chosen field. Special education teachers often find that they are supposed to fit into the professional development that is offered by their school district. They are often told to attend the class or session that makes sense when their general education counterparts have a specific place they are supposed to go.

Insufficient Support

Every teacher has pressure on their shoulders and not enough support, but in the context of a special education teacher, these individuals face even greater pressure. Moreover, these teachers face a special set of challenges due to special circumstances, which general education teachers will never understand or get because they don't have to go through them. This makes it difficult for other teachers to relate to them. School administrators also fail to support teachers in important matters.

Lack of Parent Involvement

Parents must understand that their child's special education teacher is not a fairy godmother (or a miracle worker). He or she is only human, someone who has invested his or her heart and soul, and physical capabilities toward the development of their child. Parents need to work side by side with teachers to reinforce lessons learned in the classroom. This is an obvious responsibility on the part of parents, considering students spend at least 70% of their time[46]

---

[46]NCLB Reauthorization: Effective Strategies for Engaging Parents ..., Volume 4

outside of school. They have to play their part by making sure their kids are completing homework, preparing for tests, and show interest in the class. Parents need to be actively involved in helping them overcome those difficulties at home. Additionally, parents need to become experts on a wide range of legal, medical, and educational matters that concern their child.

Overcrowded Classrooms

Students who come to a special education classroom have different ages and different disabilities. The special education teachers have their hands full, as they not only have to provide appropriate lessons for each group but also modify the lesson to fit the unique disability of each student. Budget cuts force students into a special education classroom, which makes the job difficult and stressful for the teacher because he or she is managing everything completely on his or her own.

Insufficient Remuneration

The lowest 10%, as per BLS, earned less than $37,760.[47] On the other hand, $93,090 was earned by the highest 10%. Additionally, the median annual wage, according to BLS, was $57,910 in May 2018[48]. It's this disparity in wages that force many special education teachers to quit. Another reason for quitting this field of work is the long hours and crushing paperwork[49].

All of the above are reasons parents of children needing special education need to team up with special education teachers, ensuring their children get the necessary help and the teacher can relax a bit, knowing somebody is on their side. Another reason parents need to become more proactive regarding the education of their children is the gross power imbalance. Public education is operated and controlled locally, which means every school district has its own

---

[47]https://www.bls.gov/ooh/education-training-and-library/special-education-teachers.htm#tab-5

[48]https://www.bls.gov/ooh/education-training-and-library/special-education-teachers.htm#tab-5

[49] Lee Hale, November 2015, Behind The Shortage Of Special Ed Teachers: Long Hours, Crushing Paperwork:
https://www.npr.org/sections/ed/2015/11/09/436588372/behind-the-shortage-of-special-ed-teachers-long-hours-crushing-paperwork

priorities and funding abilities. In some districts, administrators even go so far as to create specialized programs for high-need or special students; however, this isn't the case with every district.

40% of the average per-student cost was decided by the federal government to pay for every special education and needs student. This became possible after the Individuals with Disabilities Act was enacted. $7,552 is the current average per-student, whereas $9,369 per student is to be paid as the average cost per special education student.

Yet, the federal government didn't provide the entire committed amount in 2004. Just 20% was paid to local school districts, which burdened the local communities due to a shortage in the budget. This also denied full access and opportunity to all students — with and without disabilities[50].

What happens when a school is short of funds? Such budget cuts can lead to schools crowding special education classrooms and slashing resources in a bid

---

[50]http://www.nea.org/home/19029.htm

to save money. The cost of general education for a child with disabilities is twice the amount needed for a child without disabilities. Why is that so? Because many special needs children require the aid of special services during the day, and sometimes even after leaving school and for life.

However, special education programs are often not given high priority and are underfunded as a result. This ultimately leads to poor student results as well as repercussions for schools and communities. Despite all the challenges and issues mentioned above, nobody is as dedicated, honest to their work, and hardworking as a special education teacher. It's a fact: students with special needs need more attention than students without special needs, but due to obstacles, the job is one of the most stressful.

Still, a special education teacher stands by your child. Let's not forget the epic student meltdowns, which occur in the same pattern as students without disabilities and are a source of stress. Emotionally disturbed students sometimes become aggressive at their teacher and other students. A special education teacher wears many hats. He or she is more than a classroom teacher. In many scenarios, the special education teacher is a provider for services that will make your child succeed in life, and not just in school. Plenty of unofficial duties are attached to this job – a special education teacher is a coordinator and counselor and provides a sympathetic ear to parents.

There also is the challenge of managing and teaching students that have different capabilities and disabilities. Many people (parents included) assume a child in a special education class has an emotional or behavioral problem, writing off the child's potential or ability to learn. It's the hard work of special education teachers that transform children with special needs, by educating and training them according to their capabilities and going so far as assisting them outside of the classroom and sometimes after graduation from school.

These are the reasons we need to appreciate the backbone of special education, the teachers who pour their heart and soul into the cause. There are many heartfelt and genuine ways to thank a special education teacher for serving the public school system, as well as the community.

Chapter7
Instructional Assistants

"Behind every good teacher is a great instructional assistant."

–Unknown

A teacher cannot be expected to teach a classroom of 20 kids without needing assistance. This is where instructional assistants come into the picture. More commonly known as teaching assistants, these professionals are the backbone and support for the entire classroom.

An instructional assistant is primarily supposed to assist teachers in matters related to daily classroom management. Depending upon the district, the school as well as the teacher they work under, IAs can have varying roles. However, they are generally expected to work with students providing behavioral support and assisting with administrative tasks. An IA also can be called a paraeducator, which is not the same as a teacher. This means that an IA is not responsible for the learning that goes on in the classroom; that firmly remains the teacher's job. Therefore, the teacher is ultimately responsible for making sure that students are progressing with their learning, feeling adequately stimulated and safe, while also accomplishing their individualized education program (IEP) goals. Regardless, the IA constitutes an important part of the overall team because an IA can provide suitable support to the teacher and help accomplish all educational goals timely and efficiently.

To fully understand what an instructional assistant does in the classroom during a standard school day, let's consider the following:

Role of an Instructional Teacher

Most IAs work in six-hour shifts; however, their shifts may vary. A description of the average Instructional Teacher's workday is described as follows:

First Hour

The IA meets students at the bus station and accompanies them to their respective classrooms. The IA can assist in speeding up classroom activities by helping with various tasks such as putting the coats away, making the students settle down and taking roll call. During this time, the IA can complete any other administrative tasks assigned to them by the teacher.

Second Hour

During this hour, they are responsible for controlling the behavior of an assigned reading group comprising of three to five students. The reading groups follow the learning plan as designed by the teacher. The IA's workload also involves supervision during the student's independent reading time.

Third Hour

The IA is instructed to supervise a math group formed of three to five students. The instructions for the supervised group are again those as per the lesson plan supplied by the teacher. Independent learning by the kids is supervised, and one-on-one support is provided whenever necessary.

Fourth Hour

This hour is spent assisting in supervisory responsibilities outside the classroom during lunchtime and recess. The IAs typically monitor students while promoting interaction and playing with peers during unstructured time.

Fifth Hour

Additional support is provided by the IAs during all remaining hours of lessons. This can be in the form of focused assistance, control of behavioral issues in the classroom, as well as taking control of and instructing a small group of students. During this time, the IAs can venture out to other classrooms and assist them.

Sixth Hour

At the end of the day, the IA can assist with the end-of-day activities in either their assigned special education classrooms or the other general education classrooms. Finally, they accompany the kids to the bus and further provide adequate supervision for the students staying late for afterschool activities. After doing this, they often return to the classroom for any staff meetings or additional tasks assigned to them by the teacher. As we can judge, the job of an instructional assistant is a busy one and obviously very important for the teacher. However, when the teacher's workload hits an all-time high, the school support staff faces issues and struggles, which creates pressure on the entire school. The role of an instructional assistant has become increasingly demanding and difficult, which, at times, results in a negative impact on their health and well-being.

The struggles are

Challenging Pupil Behavior – Teaching assistants often work closely and one-on-one with the class's most challenging pupils, most of which are in the special education class. Constant dealing with extreme pupil behavior can become stressful.

Increasing Workload & Conflicting Demands – Workplace expectations are highly unfeasible. The biggest challenge IAs face is the issue of pressure – they have to do a million and one things that are unrealistic in a given timeframe. Failure to do all of what is expected in a given day leaves IAs feeling they have failed.

No Clear Job Description & Multiple Roles – Many IAs have shown concerns in regards to their job description… many feeling that it doesn't fit and represents only half of the work actually done in a day.

The "any other duties" part of the role is abused regularly, forcing IAs to take on a wide range of tasks, from developing the school website to organizing school trips. Low wages and consistent money worries also plague the minds of many instructional assistants, making them take second jobs or other part-time roles within the school, constantly switching between them. It's no surprise that instructional assistants often take on roles of the lollipop lady, office administrator, and lunchtime supervisor, or have duties at afterschool programs or breakfast clubs.

Unfortunately, IAs are assumed to have low status because of the roles they play, and the fact that many are now employed on insecure contracts means they may feel it's a waste of time and effort to challenge or even speak up to school administrators about these issues. However, the opposite is true. Instructional assistants are often the essence and spirit of the entire school. These professionals are the bones keeping the structure together... these are the professionals who often care for children with disabilities and tutor young readers. All the protests feature teachers demanding a fairer compensation, benefits, and representation — all other school support workers, such as the instructional assistants, remain on the sidelines and continue to show up at the schools because if they don't show up, they won't be paid. We also sometimes forget the many benefits of having an IA as well as a classroom teacher for our special kids. Each time the discussion of the education budget and its ultimate reduction is brought up, the hearts of the nation's thousands of instructional assistants plummet a little.

Far from being auxiliary classroom extras, these hardworking professionals are the lifelines for teachers and an essential element for helping achieve the full potentials of children, especially those who may need a little extra support. Here are some reasons that we need to recognize teaching assistants as the blessing they are and acknowledge their important role as part of our education system.

- **They offer individual support...** to the children who are overwhelmed in a packed classroom and unable to absorb lessons of that day. Teaching assistants play a pivotal role in providing individualized attention in reading groups. In fact, there needs to be more IAs to tackle the issue of children not having enough attention from teachers.

- **They provide access to children...** who require specialized support. Assistants are specially trained and equipped to support students with disabilities, such as physical handicaps, speech issues, behavioral problems, and a myriad of other conditions. With the presence of IAs, these children have a much better chance of accessing education.

- **They take some pressure off the teacher...** which is a good thing as handling a class of thirty children can be difficult. Teachers need all the help they can get during a difficult lesson. The help of an IA or even two IAs can help ease the load from teachers, enabling them to best provide quality education to students. IAs aren't just for the disadvantaged kids or children with special needs. These dedicated professionals can also be utilized in situations for all students.

- **They implement strategies...** when it comes to tackling the difficult kids or those who need attention. With the combined expertise and knowledge of both teachers and their assistants, it can allow the better identification of students that may require extra help or even some intervention. This can ensure that no child gets left behind or held back because all the students are well cared for and their problems are adequately addressed.

- **They are welcoming and accessible...** that does not in any way mean that the teachers are not as well. In fact, both professionals are lovely and wonderful people. However, teachers have a position of power, which can make it intimidating for parents and students to approach them. Enter the IA that is more approachable for students and make it easy for them to confide in the IA, which is a good thing.

- **They assist behind the scenes**[51]**...** so let us abandon the frivolous and false rumors of a secret army of mothers that help their

---

[51]https://www.tps.k12.mi.us/uploaded/District/IA_Manual-C2.pdf

children. Teaching assistants fully immerse themselves into students' lives and plan, assess and monitor the students to make sure that students realize their maximum potential. An IA's job is often thought to be one that starts at 9 and ends at 3, yet that isn't the case at all.

- **They can team-teach, too...** and often do! These different interactive lessons are a fun and enjoyable way for students to learn. The conventional method of holding a class can sometimes get a little monotonous. In such cases, a different approach is taken by the teachers and assistants who join forces to deliver an exciting lesson. It can be done either through an interactive method of a presentation or singing a song together. This different approach can help to keep the child focused and enthralled about learning.

This proves the IA is more than just a face or just an entity in the class. For many students, an IA is a big part of their lives who can and does have a serious impact on their future. They deserve all the support and some more that we can offer.

Yes, we do have a national teacher appreciation day (a week in some schools) in which individuals and communities across the United States are invited to recognize the importance of honoring teachers and their meaningful work. We absolutely should use this week to shower teachers with gratitude, words of encouragement, and gifts to acknowledge the amazing job they do.

Instructional assistants are invaluable assets in the classroom, without a doubt, and can help teachers in many ways. A good IA should be patient, have the required time management skills, and be able to work with a diversity of students. This is just one of the many reasons we need to applaud their involvement in the classroom and recognize dedicated IAs for their untiring efforts, to bridge the gap between the teacher, students, and the parents.

Chapter 8
Culinary & Facilities Staff

"Thank you so much for the lunches. I need a lunch because we don't have lunch stuff at home. Lunch tastes good!"

– 5th Grade Student

Do you remember standing in line at the school cafeteria, waiting for an unappetizing piece of tough chicken or a barely chewable slice of pepperoni pizza? Fast-forward to now, and you might be wondering whether or not the state of school lunches has improved since your time in school.

Here Is How Schools Feed Their Students

Planning daily school meals is a very complicated process. The menus need to be designed, keeping in mind the various tastes and dietary restrictions of each kid. School meals need to cater to the children who might have some food allergies, such as lactose intolerance, peanut allergies.

Additionally, they also have a very limited budget when it comes to feeding students, not just delicious but also healthy food. So, what does that mean? All school food needs to be made at a lower cost and not require too much preparation, which means the food served in school canteens and cafeterias is often high in sugar, fat, and salt.

Consider all the students who attend public schools in the United States. Healthy food is a large part of their development, and it is estimated that kids eat about 35% and 40%[52] of their daily caloric intake during their time at school. This means that it's extremely important for this daily food intake to be healthy in nature.

However, unfortunately, most of these calories are unhealthy and can be divided into three main categories:

- Daily school meals like breakfast, lunch, and after-school snacks – Funded by the U.S. Department of Agriculture, the total

---

[52]Are School Lunches Really Important for your Kid's Health: https://health.ucdavis.edu/good-food/blog/school-lunches-and-kids.html

expenditure amounts to about $13 billion[53] each year.

- The food and drink items – These are sold in vending machines are also found in the cafeteria at schools and often have higher fat content. There are more empty calories consumed, as well.

- Outside snacks and foods – These are brought in by students for snacking upon or as a lunch. Food is also brought in for birthdays, school fundraisers, and sporting events.

Regulations Regarding School Lunches

Lunchtime is undoubtedly the most important meal of the day, especially for children who suffer from food insecurity, i.e., who don't have access to healthy food at home. Food insecurity is described as not having reliable access to healthy and nourishing food in a generous quantity. This is one reason why meals served in schools must follow strict guidelines for healthy eating. Many of the foods, therefore, don't

---

[53] https://www.fns.usda.gov/nslp

contain more than 30% of caloric content from fat and contain no more than 10% from saturated fat. In addition, the school menu guidelines encourage the inclusion of fruits, vegetables as well as grains with the aim of enforcing more balanced food intakes.

The meals also try to reduce the overall fat content in other ways, such as by serving more vegetable options and limiting the beef, pork, and fried food options. In this way, children are encouraged to eat healthy from an early age. Healthy eating habits must be established early, but the purpose of this is not just for the avoidance of diseases such as cardiovascular problems, type 2 diabetes, and cancer in the future… it's also about ensuring the healthy food intake of children in the present.

This entails providing children with healthy meals as part of their school food intake that can ultimately allow them to better apply themselves to their academic tasks and also build their immune systems to allow maximized learning by minimized sick absences. Healthy foods thus result in healthier and smarter kids.

Just as soldiers are at the front line of defense and offense in the battlefield, doctors, and nurses, the first responders in an epidemic… the school's culinary staff are the ones responsible for providing children with healthy and delicious lunches.

Duties of Culinary Staff

The task of providing a meal every day that is not only nutritious but tasty and strike the perfect balance can be challenging every day. The number of restaurants that can provide healthy and nutritious meals with proper portions at economical pricing is limited. Furthermore, if students can not cover the cost of their meals at school, the school has provisions to allow the student to 'charge' their meal and pay it back the next day or whenever it is feasible for them.

A school cafeteria aims to nourish students via healthier meals so they can fully achieve their academic potentials and become the leaders of tomorrow. This is not only out of love but is also an important consideration.

Children, especially students, must have a well-balanced healthy and nutritious diet. In fact, students that are well-nourished perform and learn better at school. There is a directly proportional link between healthy meals and higher grades. In fact, well-nourished students are expected to have better memory and alertness, as well as faster information processing.[54]

This is one of the many reasons school districts now appoint professional culinary and relevant facilities staff, thereby ensuring students receive the proper nutrition as required by state nutrition standards. The lunch lady, often found at the bottom of the school hierarchy, is actually the most important one in this sense.

Cook – A cook has two main responsibilities. Prepping, cooking as well as serving the food meant to cater to the entire student body. Additionally, a cook is also responsible for the clean-up of both the kitchen and cafeteria at the end of the workday.

School Nutritionist– This professional is responsible for creating the official school meal plan that adequately meets the requirements of both the school and the state in terms of nutrition standards for

---

[54] Lee Watanabe-Crockett, August 2016, Good School Nutrition Can Boost Students' Performance: https://www.wabisabilearning.com/blog/good-school-nutrition-boosts-performance

each meal provided. The school nutritionist is also in charge of deciding what sort of food will be served. Their job also includes collecting the money from the students and keeping track of all the finances used by the school's nutrition programs. Additionally, the nutritionist is also responsible for keeping an eye on the students' food intake and be vigilant in noticing which students are eating and which students are not, along with the students who qualify for free or reduced-price lunches.

Cafeteria Manager & Worker – All the people that enjoy working for the betterment of children but do not have the patience to directly deal with children as teachers can consider working in school cafeterias. What is the job of these cafeteria workers? They serve meals to students during the duration of the school years. Sometimes, during the summer months, they also provide meals to children in economically disadvantaged families as part of the federal meal provision programs. These workers are just some of the people that work together in the system to fully assist children to have a proper education.

These cafeteria workers work in harmony with the teachers, teaching assistants, librarians, coaches, and counselors, as well as other staff members, to maximize the benefits children can get in their school years. The cafeteria manager is meant to make sure that the cafeteria workers have the necessary items such as food and other supplies that are required to properly serve the foods as dictated by the menu. On the other hand, it's the job of the cafeteria workers to frequently check the inventory of food and supplies and inform managers when running short of any items.

Physical labor also is part of the job description because the duties usually involve shifting large boxes and heavy equipment. The workers must also keep sanitation and cross-contamination in mind. All workers are mandated to wear protective clothing such as gloves, hairnets, and change them every few hours, especially the gloves.

The cafeteria workers also ensure that the daily equipment, kitchen spaces, long with the cafeteria itself, are routinely cleaned. They also end up performing cashier duties because they are responsible for taking payments from the children for their meals and making other appropriate changes. A cafeteria worker needs to be made aware of which children in the school are eligible for free or reduced-price meals so they can make sure those children can receive them.

Difficulties Faced By Culinary Staff

There are some unique difficulties faced by the culinary staff of schools. Everybody has this perception that the job of a cafeteria worker and other culinary staff members are the easiest jobs in a school. After all, what do they need to do other than dole out lunches on the plates and trays of hungry students and then clean up? Cafeteria staff all over the country beg to differ. They're hungry for change inside the cafeteria, especially how this unit in a school operates in a day.

The first concern cafeteria workers have regarding their job is the quality of food served to students for breakfast and lunch. A lunchroom workers union based in Chicago recently marched at the Chicago Public Schools' headquarters armed with signs and hairnets. What were they protesting? This march followed an extensive report that surveyed the self-described "lunch ladies" or workers who serve meals in schools.[55]The survey asked 436 experienced lunchroom or cafeteria workers about new changes that had been implemented in Chicago's Public Schools. The changes implemented were geared toward meeting the goal of providing healthy, nutritious, and appetizing meals that would ultimately contribute to the success of the children in the learning environment.

What were the results of the survey? A majority of cafeteria workers felt that the kids weren't eating the new, healthier food that had been mandated by the CPS. Half of the survey's respondents revealed that they "rarely or never" saw the school's Principal eating the lunches served by the cafeteria, the same meals everyone else at the school eats.

In addition, even though the cafeteria workers and culinary staff in schools support healthier school lunches, 75% of the lunch ladies said that they had little to no input in the new menus and recipes. Yes, the job description above of the cafeteria workers and the lunch ladies is misleading, considering the staff in

---

[55]http://del.h-cdn.co/assets/cm/15/10/54f944aa1bf70_-_realfoodrealjobs_CPS_Report.pdf

a school cafeteria isn't responsible for actually planning the menus and dishes. Perhaps this is why the role of the lunch lady is reduced to a woman doling out mashed potatoes and saving an extra juice box for the favorite student (although this is shown only in movies). Just like cafeteria workers and culinary staff in Chicago public schools, lunch ladies across the nation feel they don't have the authority to offer input or assistance in meal planning.

Another issue faced by the culinary staff is that of frozen food. According to the report, some cafeteria staff only reheat the frozen lunch meals they are given (this is referred to as the frozen cooking method). This means any or at all actual cooking doesn't take place in the cafeteria kitchen.

Food cooked in school from scratch is far superior as compared to reheated food, which is the general belief of 73% of the lunch ladies surveyed for the report. However, many public school districts prohibit change when it comes to the building of working kitchens in elementary schools, which means schools have no choice but to utilize the frozen cooking method as opposed to making freshly cooked and unprocessed meals in the cafeteria kitchen.[56] The last and just as important point in the survey[57] states that more than half of the lunchroom workers desired more training regarding healthy foods that are or would be part of the new menus. Public schools have been aiming for a change in regard to the food, encouraging that the food be cooked from scratch in the school kitchen.

Yet, this change requires an overhaul of changes in the existing school cafeteria's infrastructure to support the new policy. This also is why cafeteria workers and other important staff members should know or have input regarding the menu planning, because, at the end of the day, they will be responsible for making the food and ensuring the kids eat. Food wastage also is a concern shared by many lunchroom ladies across the country. Research has shown that the Lunch Program serves around thirty million kids each day. However, it also ends up wasting about $5 million worth of

---

[56] May 2015, How School Facilities Support Healthy School Food: https://healthyschoolscampaign.org/policy/how-school-facilities-support-healthy-school-food/
[57] http://del.h-cdn.co/assets/cm/15/10/54f944aa1bf70_-_realfoodrealjobs_CPS_Report.pdf

food![58] This constitutes about $1.2 billion in losses per school year.[59] These losses cannot be justified, and to make matters worse, this tacitly teaches children that it is considered acceptable to waste all their untouched food, such as ravioli and chicken tenders.

The question arises, why are schools wasting so much food? Many factors can be taken into consideration. For example, due to the lack of proper funding by the USDA and a consequential lack of proper cooking sites, the quality of food can be significantly reduced. Another factor is the USDA reimbursement requirement.

Students are encouraged to pick lunch items from three of the five categories offered, out of which at least one of those categories has little choice but to pick the food they might not even want to eat, which results in food wastage. It makes sense in theory that an excess of food choices would reduce waste.

---

[58] Jonathan Bloom, November 2018, Waste Not, Want Not: https://grist.org/article/schools-waste-5-million-a-day-in-uneaten-food-heres-how-oakland-is-reinventing-the-cafeteria/
[59] February 2013, School lunch waste among middle school students: nutrients consumed and costs: https://www.ncbi.nlm.nih.gov/pubmed/23332326

However, students aren't given a choice to pick the items they could reasonably eat and finish. But instead, the staff relying on the Federal government's "reimbursable meals" persuades the students to take more. Attached to this is the hesitance many students have when it comes to eating certain food items. Cafeteria workers and lunchroom ladies reckon that the key part when it comes to introducing new food to kids is being able to educate them regarding the healthier choices available on the menu.

For example, hummus is a dish that many kids will be wary of eating. Even though this delicious chickpea and olive oil dish offers numerous health benefits, kids still won't touch it, which means the food item will be wasted. If only cafeteria workers had the authority to conduct a class on the health benefits of the foods to be served to students on a certain day, much of the waste could be prevented.

Many school cafeteria cooks do their part in preventing wastage by making food look more appetizing. They have all kinds of tricks up their sleeves, such as cutting boring vegetables into fun shapes or "blushing the pears" by sprinkling a little powdered gelatin dessert on top so that kids can be attracted enough to eat the food. In short, anything to stop food wastage. This just proves how much the school culinary staff and cafeteria workers love their jobs. Unlike the cranky lunch lady we see in cartoons on TV, most people working in a school cafeteria do their work because they enjoy interacting with the students. It's the one reason why they get up every morning and go to work.

They would enjoy this job even more if the issues mentioned earlier are eradicated. Until then, please make their jobs even more fun... appreciate these hard workers for the angels they are.

Chapter 9
School Resource Officer

"Some of the school districts in my congressional district are looking at resource officers and how they secure that environment."

–Marsha Blackburn

A school is not the place for armed men and women to be patrolling in case of a school shooting. Yet, with hundreds of school shootings nationwide during the past decade, some believe schools need armed men and women to protect students and staff. This is the job of the school resource officer, which will be covered later in the chapter.

The situation has become worse. . . so bad that in just 46 weeks in 2018, there were 45 school shootings. That's nearly an average of one school shooting in a week. They have taken place across the country, from Georgia to California. Shootings have occurred in elementary, middle, and high schools, as well as on college and university campuses. Of those, 32 of them occurred at educational facilities having kindergarten through 12th grade.[60] The need for school safety is paramount and felt more than ever. A school resource officer is a professional who is equipped with the training required to keep a school safe and secure from school shootings and other threats. However, this isn't the only job these men and women perform for the school they've been assigned.

Duties of a School Resource Officer

It's a sad reality that schools and other educational institutions would require security and protection today, which is provided by a school resource officer. An SRO is basically a police officer who works in a school setting, whether it be elementary, middle, or high schools. This professional is responsible for developing comprehensive plans by collaborating with school admins, security staff, and school faculty — ensuring schools are safe places for students to learn and teachers to teach. In essence... a school resource officer is given the responsibility of the main security

---

[60]Elizabeth Wolfe and Christina Walker, November 2019, In 46 weeks this year, there have been 45 school shootings: https://edition.cnn.com/2019/11/15/us/2019-us-school-shootings-trnd/index.html

body of their schools. Yet, this isn't the only job these professionals perform. The complete and thorough job description includes much more than simply policing school grounds. Following are some jobs they perform that are equally important:

Safety protocols are followed by schools, which make sure students and staff remain secure and safe from harm. A safety protocol might include fire and active shooter drills, which are developed and conducted by the SRO.

Who do you think mediates between internal disputes between the students and even the staff? The SRO is the first one to break up fights in the school. Through various tactics, the SRO is able to de-escalate aggressions that might take place on school premises.

An SRO can detain or arrest an offender for breaking the law. This important job ensures that law and order are sustained within school premises.

An SRO has the authority to conduct personal, and property searches of any student he or she suspects may have broken the law. The searches include physical searches, backpack, and vehicle or locker searches.

Additionally, SRO duties may include being asked to educate teachers and staff about various safety precautions and dangers.[61] The job portfolio of an SRO is never-ending. Depending on the situation, an SRO protects against theft and property damage, as well as assisting in medical emergencies. In short, they do everything in their power to reduce incidents that warrant a call to and intervention from 911.

Even More Need for Security Resource Officers Today

The first adult that millions of students see and get greeted by isn't a teacher or the Principal. The first adult that students see is a school resource officer, which is overlooked in law enforcement. To make matters worse for these dedicated and reliable professionals, what a security resource officer should do has come under the national glare in recent years. In a nutshell, the job and duties of a school resource officer range from easy to difficult. SROs may be needed to perk up sullen and scared students, direct

---

[61]The Role of a School Resource Officer:
http://cte.jhu.edu/courses/ssn/sro/ses1_act4_pag1.shtml

bus traffic, settle disputes, or keep a watchful eye out for threats. Although the position has a genial-sounding name, the duties consist of an unusual hybrid – on any given day, the SRO of a school may act the role of a cop holding hands with a counselor. Perhaps no other job shows America's shifting ideas about schools, as well as policing and safety issues better than SROs.

The number of SROs increased after the 1999 Columbine High School shooting.[62] In New York City, for example, every school has one SRO stationed at school premises. These SROs, although unarmed, have the power to make arrests as they are employed by the New York Police Department. Certain schools in the city can also have armed SROS on their premises, assigned by the department.

Is it an easy job? Not even close. Even in the best of scenarios, the job of an SRO isn't an easy one to fill, especially considering that most cops don't particularly like to be assigned at a school, because they didn't join law enforcement for this reason. They

---

[62]https://www.nytimes.com/topic/organization/columbine-high-school

want to be on the streets, keeping the peace, and catching law-breaking citizens. This is one issue that has fed the existing stereotype that SROs aren't the best of the best in their department and are "demoted" to this position.[63] The opposite is true. School resource officers are the first line of defense if things go south, and they are the real heroes.

They have to perform all the above-mentioned roles as well as ensure the biggest responsibility is taken care of, yet SROs don't receive anything more than the most basic training given to other officers. This is why school resource officers often draw on their empathy and listening skills. How does this help? Doing good in their job actually requires the SRO to understand troubled young people and children and build strong relationships with them.

This makes the role a community-based policing approach. In its essence, it's about three essential components. The first one is problem-solving, every SRO has to come up with solutions on the mark.

---

[63]https://www.nytimes.com/2018/03/04/us/school-resource-officers-shooting.html

Relationship building comes next, which is important as young people begin to trust the SRO. The third is doing everything in power to make a positive difference and change in their lives. The dangers of the job (getting shot is just one) don't stop these brave men and women from becoming the first line of defense for a school and its inhabitants. If they were asked why they do the job they do, many would say they do it for the students, to let them know someone is keeping them safe.

Just as teachers and school counselors are responsible for helping disadvantaged students, the role of an SRO. Stress, neglect, abuse, and absenteeism takes a huge chunk out of what could have been a child's development. Many then grow up to be impulsive risk-takers and get in a lot of trouble in school and outside.[64] This is why a compassionate, children-caring, and emphatic SRO comes in the picture, Two SROs at a Weston, Florida, school[65]show why they help school kids, especially the ones coming

---

[64] Ian Chant, January 2013, Troubled Family Life Changes Kids Brains: https://www.scientificamerican.com/article/troubled-family-life-changes-kids-b/
[65] Ted Craft, July 2019, School Resource Officers: Key to Truly Safe Schools: https://westontoday.news/articles/190704-sros

from disturbed families. Sometimes, the SROs learn of possible family issues as a result of police calls about domestic incidents. In many cases, schools aren't aware of problems at a child's home because disclosing information violates their rights and privacy. In such a scenario, there's not much that can be done except increase interaction with the troubled kid, keep an eye out for signs of trouble (like bad grades, truancy or substance abuse) and generally be there for help and support.

In many instances, the kids are involved in incidents that aren't criminal offenses but are scenarios in which the SRO can intervene to help. What is an example of such an intervention? The student may be doing inappropriate things on social media, forcing the SRO to step in, contact the parent sand counsel the kid. None of this could happen if the SRO isn't on campus and unable to make a connection and relationship with the students. Without this, one cannot understand what kids are up to, what's important to them, how they socialize, what music they like, or how they communicate. The school resource officers in the Weston school are aware of people. They aren't the parents of the students, or the teachers and administrators. They aren't even guidance counselors or psychologists. In fact, they are a bit of everything. In a time of mass hysteria and school shootings taking place every other week, isn't it time we should appreciate school resource officers for the heroes they are? As I have stated, police officers, first responders, EMT's, firefighters, and our military personnel are always our heroes, right? From my experience, it doesn't take much to bring a smile to their faces... and they already know the job and position is worth it.

But a little appreciation doesn't hurt. Say thanks to your kid's school resource officer, bring him or her a muffin and coffee (or tea), have your kid make the officer a handmade card. It's the little things that make a job truly wonderful. Remember, the people who work in the public school system REALLY CARE, which is why they come to work every day despite the low pay. Why? They do this because they want to contribute to society positively.

Chapter 10
Conclusion

"Appreciation is a wonderful thing. It makes what is excellent in others belong to us as well."

-Voltaire

What did the previous chapters tell us? It can be tough to work in a public school, in whichever position. Teachers, Principals, and all other professionals involved in the effective operation of a school perform their duties and responsibilities diligently, most of the time, without recognition or appreciation.

It's about time the school staff and personnel receive the recognition and appreciation they rightfully deserve, especially those who leave behind life-affirming legacies, such as the Principal at Farmington Junior High School in Utah.[66] According

---

[66]Amy K. Stewart, December 2009, Farmington Jr. Principal left legacy to teens, teachers:
https://www.deseret.com/2009/12/9/20357565/farmington-jr-Principal-left-legacy-to-teens-teachers

to students and school staff, the Principal - who died after a long battle with cancer – all say he left a long-lasting impression on the life of students. He was known for his reasonable attitude, kind sense of humor, and his devotion towards his family and his military service. A ninth-grader eulogized him in these words, *"He was an example of leadership and had a positive attitude, clear to the end."*

Teachers are honored for their service and duty each year in the month of May by the U.S. schools. A Teacher Appreciation Week is celebrated in all the schools, private or public across the country. World Teacher's Day is celebrated all over the world on October 5. This makes one think that teachers are appreciated for the work that they do, for our children and youth, the ways they positively touch and inspire them.

After all, it's the efforts of a teacher that act as a foundation-stone on which lies the nation's future. So, I am speaking to all of you — teachers, administrators, Principals, substitute, instructional and special education teachers, support and culinary staff, school resource officers – we thank you!

How to Show Thanks to Those Unsung Heroes

It doesn't matter how you decide to and show thanks to these hardworking and dedicated professionals. Any and every effort is welcome and will be appreciated by them! So what is important? The essential thing is to SHOW them your appreciation. There are many reasons to appreciate someone for a job well done, especially if that job is in the public education system.

Valued and respected teachers and other school staff will be more productive and happier when performing their respective duties, which will make them more effective and efficient professionals. This leads to the students being successful. Just like our veterans and soldiers, it's very easy for us to recognize our nation's teachers, to some extent.

However, the fact of the matter is that most are underpaid and still very much underappreciated. Surprising, isn't it? Especially considering how much-dedicated school personnel is when it comes to shaping the future aspirations and goals of the children and youth. So yes, these wonderful people deserve honor, respect, and loads of appreciation — more than double the amount. This includes substitute teachers — the backup when the main classroom teacher cannot attend school and teach the children. We think their job is easy... it's anything but easy, but we can at least make it a little more bearable. Next in line comes instructional assistants and special education teachers. It's through their dedication and concentrated efforts that special needs kids and those that require more help are able to do well in their studies.

A special round of recognition and appreciation needs to be given for our school support staff – the resource officer and culinary staff. One takes care of the safety and security of our children while the second fights for them to receive nutritious meals.

However, another group works tirelessly behind the scenes at every school in the country. They are also incredibly overworked and underappreciated. Do they receive the recognition deserved? No. Who are these people? There are our school administrators.

They conduct highly crucial tasks for salaries don't even compare to their private-sector counterparts. Let's just take the example of teachers to prove this point.

A recent version of NEAs Rankings and Estimates show $59,660 is the average nationwide salary of a teacher. However, the economic conditions have worsened over the years, and this means that a teacher's position has also declined financially. Inflation is the biggest contributor to this erosion, which reduces the amount to $1,823 despite witnessing an increase of average salary by 15.2%.

On the other hand, professionals that have a similar education level actually earn higher salaries as compared to teachers. According to the Economic Policy Institute, teachers earn 19% less than professionals that have similar skills and education level. Known as the "teaching penalty," this unfairness has increased from 2% to 19%.[67]

Recognizing What Each Does

It's important to appreciate what school administrators do for their schools. It's important to understand what they contribute to the process. Only then can we fully support education. So let's take a

---

[67] September 2018, Teacher Compensation: Fact vs. Fiction:http://www.nea.org/home/12661.htm

moment to say thank you for doing all of this and more. Thank you for being the first to arrive each morning and the last to leave after everyone.

What do they do? Effective school administrators:

- Clear the path of obstacles and hurdles and hindrances in front teachers, which makes it easier for them to reach out to students and effectively teach them.

- Help teachers find and make use of opportunities to hone their teaching skills and develop new ones.

- Often parents of students have unfair and unrealistic expectations from teachers when it comes to the child's education. The school admin supports and encourages teachers in this area as well.

- They help to manage the fiscal and physical resources available to the school. They make it a point to take on the burden of resource allocation so that teachers can focus on teaching and empowering learners.

With a heart full of gratitude... Thank you! Why should we thank superintendents? These individuals are responsible for creating an environment that nurtures lifelong learning in our children.

They:

- Manage and lead all schools in their district, despite receiving a very low and limited budget.
- Comply with ever-increasingly and complex compliance regulations.

With a heart full of gratitude... Thank you!

What do the Principals do in a school? They do an important job – these individuals, with the help of the assistant Principal, take care of every detail that involves the operation of a school. In addition, a good Principal supports teachers, creating a safe and positive environment for the teachers and students. To summarize their contribution to education and society, they:

- Make sure that the curriculum is followed and maintained as well as education standards. They also make sure the methods used by teachers are effective.
- Manage the professional development of the teaching staff.

- Provide support for the teachers facing discipline issues with the students.

With a heart full of gratitude... Thank you!

Next, come the school support staff. These workers represented more than 40% of public school employees in the country. They are the secretaries, teacher aides, cafeteria workers, bus drivers, maintenance workers, and groundskeepers.[68] These people are the backbone of every school, the ones who work behind the scenes and ensure the machinery operates smoothly so that the teachers and Principals can do their jobs in a better manner.

For the dedication and commitment that you have shown to our schools, teachers and staff, and students – we thank you. Your professionalism is appreciated. Your compassion is valued. Your commitment to this noble profession is recognized.

"The deepest principle of human nature is a craving to be appreciated."

–William James

---

[68] https://nces.ed.gov/programs/digest/d17/tables/dt17_213.10.asp?Current=yes

Everyone feels the need to be recognized and appreciated for the hard work they put into something they love doing because the feeling of being appreciated enables people to persevere through the bad days at work. The truth is, all of us want to be recognized; all of us need to feel that we are valued — for who we are and what we do. We need to be appreciated and recognized for our accomplishments and contributions, in whatever capacity, level, and importance.

We need to know that we have made a difference in someone's life. After all, isn't the same thinking shared by employees of private companies? People expect a "Best Employee of the Month: reward if they hit the highest target or make the most sales. Why then, do we not provide the same to teachers and other individuals who are closely connected with the public education system of this country?

PHILIP BRENT GONZALEZ